SPEC...

The Batman jerk... ... ...obby, but he saw the big Grizzly coming up and barely had time to wrap his Kevlar-paneled cape around himself before it went off. The big .45 Magnum slug struck the Kevlar panels in his cape, but they were not strong enough to withstand such a powerful round. The bullet penetrated, but was sufficiently slowed that the protective bat emblem on his chest was able to stop it. However, there was no doing anything about the impact. The 230-grain jacketed bullet traveling at over 1600 feet per second packed a wallop that knocked him right off his feet, stunning him.

Specter holstered the pistol and picked up the assault rifle, with its larger magazine of high-velocity .223 ammo. The light from the flare pellets was now almost completely gone. As the Batman lay stunned, Specter activated the laser sight and placed the red dot of the beam right over the Batman's belly.

"I've got about thirty rounds left," he said with a cold smile. "Let's see how many you can take before you die."

★

BATMAN:
TO STALK A SPECTER

RoC

**Exploring New Realms
in Science Fiction/Fantasy Adventure**

Calling all fantasy fans!

Join the

RoC

FANTASY FAN CLUB
for exciting news and fabulous competitions.

For further information write to:

RoC

FANTASY FAN CLUB
Penguin Books Ltd.,
Bath Road, Harmondsworth,
Middlesex UB7 0DA

Open only to residents of the UK
and Republic of Ireland

BATMAN™:
TO STALK A SPECTER

SIMON HAWKE

A ROC BOOK

ROC

Published by the Penguin Group
Penguin Books Ltd, 27 Wrights Lane, London W8 5TZ, England
Penguin Books USA Inc., 375 Hudson Street, New York, New York 10014, USA
Penguin Books Australia Ltd, Ringwood, Victoria, Australia
Penguin Books Canada Ltd, 10 Alcorn Avenue, Toronto, Ontario, Canada M4V 3B2
Penguin Books (NZ) Ltd, 182–190 Wairau Road, Auckland 10, New Zealand

Penguin Books Ltd, Registered Offices: Harmondsworth, Middlesex, England

First published in the USA by Warner Books, Inc., a Time Warner Company, 1991
Published in Penguin Books 1991
1 3 5 7 9 10 8 6 4 2

Copyright © DC Comics, Inc., 1991
All rights reserved

The moral right of the author has been asserted

All characters, their distinctive likenesses and all related indicia
are trademarks of DC Comics, Inc.

ROC is an imprint of Penguin Books Ltd

Printed in England by Clays Ltd, St Ives plc

Except in the United States of America, this book is sold subject
to the condition that it shall not, by way of trade or otherwise, be lent,
re-sold, hired out, or otherwise circulated without the publisher's
prior consent in any form of binding or cover other than that in
which it is published and without a similar condition including this
condition being imposed on the subsequent purchaser

Dedicated to Cass Marshall,
with gratitude for the friendship
and encouragement

PROLOGUE

"EXCUSE me, Ambassador," said the maître d', as he came up to the table. "There's a telephone call for you, sir. The gentleman did not identify himself, but he said it was important. Do you wish to take the call?"

"Yes, thank you, Phillipe. I'll take it."

The maître d' handed him a remote phone handset.

The ambassador turned to his lunch companions and said, "Please excuse me for a moment," then put the handset to his ear and identified himself.

"You requested my services," the caller said, speaking with a Continental accent. "There is a telephone stall across the street. Go there now, please."

The connection was abruptly broken.

The ambassador made a pretense that there was still someone on the line. "Yes, I see," he said. "No, no, I understand. I will have to see to it myself. I will be there directly." He handed the phone back to the maître d', turned to his companions, and said, "I fear something has come up at the embassy that requires my immediate attention."

His companions assured him that they understood, and he excused himself and left the restaurant. He stood on the sidewalk for a moment, waiting for a break in the busy lunch-hour traffic, then quickly crossed the street to the phone stall opposite the restaurant. He walked up to the stall, looked around briefly, and waited. A moment later, he heard someone behind him shout, "Hey, why don't you watch where the hell you're going?"

"Up yours, buddy."

"*What* did you say to me?"

"You heard me. I said, up yours!"

Behind him, two men were squared off in a confrontation on the sidewalk. The phone rang. He picked it up at once.

"This is Specter," said the voice with the Continental accent.

The ambassador glanced around nervously. The two men behind him were shouting at each other loudly and looked as if they were about to come to blows.

"The argument is merely a diversion to mask our conversation from any microphones in the vicinity," said the man who called himself Specter. "Forgive the elaborate precautions, but you are known to frequent that particular restaurant, and its lines might have been tapped."

"You are a very careful man," the ambassador said.

"The nature of my work requires caution. I have decided to accept the contract."

Behind the ambassador, the argument was heating up and a crowd was gathering.

"The fee will be one million dollars in U.S. currency," said Specter.

"One million!" the ambassador said with disbelief.

"It is non-negotiable. You will be contacted for the payment at your embassy reception next Friday. The contact shall be a blond woman, wearing a black velvet cocktail dress with a diamond, star-shaped brooch. You will compliment her on the dress and ask if it is a designer original. She will respond by saying, 'Believe it or not, I made it myself from a pattern in a magazine,' and she will wink at you."

"You expect me to turn one million dollars over to her at the *reception*?" said the ambassador, astonished.

"Of course not. You will be seen flirting with her. She will make it easy for you. You will leave the reception with her and she will accompany you home, where you will deliver the money, in packets of one-hundred-dollar bills. For the sake of appearances, she will remain with you for several hours, then you will send her home in your car. She will instruct the driver where to let her out. As this will not be an unusual pattern of behavior for you, it should arouse no suspicion in the event that you are being watched."

"I *beg* your pardon!" protested the ambassador. "How would *you* know about—" But the man had already hung up.

"Don't you push me!"

"Why, what're you gonna *do* about it, jerk?"

"Who you callin' a jerk?"

"I'm callin' *you* a jerk, you jerk!"

"Get your damn hands off me! You push me one more time and so help me, I'll..."

"You'll *what*? Come on, you want a piece of me? Come on! *Put 'em up!*"

"All right, break it up, break it up," said a cop, pushing his way through the crowd.

The ambassador hung up the phone and quickly crossed the street, heading toward his waiting embassy car. The two antagonists on the sidewalk instantly calmed down in the presence of the police officer and, after a few admonishing words from him, went their separate ways. The crowd dispersed.

"You get anything?" said the federal agent in the car across the street.

His partner took off his headphones, lowered the small dish mike, and shook his head. "What, with all that noise? Forget it. I couldn't make out a thing."

"Terrific. You think it was a setup?"

"Nah, he was probably just calling some bimbo. Didn't want to do it from the restaurant, where he could be overheard. Hell, it wouldn't be the first time."

"Why didn't he just use his car phone?"

"Hmm. Good question."

"You got a good answer?"

"Nope."

"Neither do I."

"You don't suppose he spotted us?"

"I don't know." The agent reached for the cellular phone. "I don't like it. There's something going on."

"You think it's about Garcia?"

"I *don't* think it's about some bimbo." He spoke into the phone. "This is Jernigan. Put me through to Chambers."

CHAPTER ONE

"GOOD evening. This is Roger Greeley, and here is tonight's news. The controversy over the arrest of Latin American strongman Desiderio Garcia continues unabated. At a press conference earlier this afternoon, the White House made its first official response to the protests over the capture of General Garcia. For details on that story, we go to Connie Williams, in Washington."

The camera cut to an attractive, dark-haired, extremely well-groomed woman standing on the stairs in front of the State Department building.

"Roger, for the first time since the daring midnight raid on the private fortress villa of General Desiderio Garcia by a crack team of Delta Force commandos and agents of the CIA, the White House has issued a statement in reply to protests lodged by several foreign governments concerning the manner of General Garcia's capture. At four o'clock this afternoon, White House Press Secretary Walter Davies made a short statement concerning the arrest of General Garcia and then took questions from the White House press corps."

The camera cut to a tape of the press conference. Press Secretary Davies, a heavy-set, balding man in a dark blue suit, stood behind a bank of microphones at the podium.

"Good evening, ladies and gentlemen," he said. "I will read a short statement, and then I will take your questions. 'It is the position of the government of the United States that the arrest of General Garcia was conducted in a manner according to our laws and was entirely justified. In addition to illegally nullifying the free and democratic elections of his country, General Garcia is, and has been for quite some time, an international drug trafficker, with known connections to a number of terrorist organizations, which he has not only supported with arms and funds from his traffic in cocaine, but also provided with bases for use as training camps. His arrest was executed in accordance with a federal warrant, citing his drug smuggling and terrorist activities, as well as his direct involvement in a plot involving a planned assassination attempt against a number of delegates to the United Nations. Pending his trial in federal court at Gotham City, General Garcia will be accorded the same rights and legal representation as any American citizen, under due process of law.' That concludes the statement. I will take your questions now."

"Mr. Davies, has the President made any response to the protests from the Soviet Union, Cuba, and a number of the Mideast countries?"

"The President's position on the matter is reflected by the statement I've just read," Davies replied.

"What about the claim that General Garcia was seized illegally, kidnapped on his own soil?"

"Our laws give us the right to execute federal warrants on foreign soil when it concerns terrorists who pose a threat to the security of the people and government of the United States," said Davies.

"What about the opinion of the World Court?"

"It is just that, Sam, an opinion. We are not legally bound by it."

"Does the government have any documented proof of General Garcia's involvement in drug traffic?"

"We feel that we have ample evidence that will stand up in a court of law," said Davies.

"What about this alleged assassination plot? Can you give us any more details? Who, specifically, were the targets, and how does General Garcia tie into it?"

"I am not, at this moment, at liberty to go into that," said Davies.

"But you said he was directly involved."

"That is correct. We have evidence of that."

"What form of evidence?"

"I am not at liberty to say."

"Does the government have a witness?"

"I believe I've already answered that question."

"What about international opinion?"

"Great Britain has expressed support of our action," Davies replied, "saying that it was fully justified, and we have received statements of support from the governments of Canada, Australia, France, and a number of other nations as well. I might also add that we have overwhelming support from the American people."

"Mr. Davies, in light of the protest from the Soviet Union, do you think this will affect the upcoming summit and our growing relations with that country?"

"A great deal of that will depend on them, but no, I do not believe it will."

"What about the general's claim, as reported by his attorneys, that as someone who is not a citizen of the United States, he isn't subject to our laws?"

"General Garcia is entitled to claim anything he wants," said Davies. "The matter will be up to the courts to decide. Thank you very much. That will be all for now."

There were several more shouted questions, but Davies ignored them and left the podium. The camera cut back to Connie Williams.

"Press Secretary Davies left a number of key questions unanswered," she said, "such as the details of the alleged assassination plot against members of the UN and the specific nature of the evidence the government has against General Garcia. It would be logical to assume that the government has at least one witness who can testify to these allegations, but Mr. Davies did not confirm or deny that. As for the popular support that Secretary Davies cited, according to our own poll, that support is, indeed, overwhelming. When asked if they supported the actions of the government in the arrest of General Garcia, sixty-eight percent of those polled said yes, ten percent said no, and twenty-two percent had no opinion. Reporting from the State Department, this is Connie Williams."

The camera cut back to the anchorman. "In other news tonight, an autopsy confirmed drug overdose as the cause of death in All-American running back and Heisman Trophy winner John Maslowitz—"

Bruce Wayne hit the off button on the remote control and the TV set fell silent. He sat back in his chair and sighed. Whatever happened, he wondered, to the days of clean-cut college athletes whose worst overindulgence might be a few too many beers at a frat party? Kids were dying of drug abuse, and one of the most infamous drug lords in the world—and a terrorist to boot—was finally being brought to justice, yet twenty-two percent of the citizens polled had no opinion on the matter. Amazing. How could anyone have no opinion?

"Dinner is ready, Master Bruce," said Alfred Pennyworth.

"No, thank you, Alfred. I'm not hungry."

"Is there something wrong, sir?"

The Batman looked up at the butler and grimaced wryly. "There's always something wrong somewhere, Alfred. It's just that lately, there seems to be more and more of it."

"Yes, sir. I quite understand. But you really should eat something, sir. I can hardly recommend swinging from the rooftops on an empty stomach."

He had to smile. It never ceased to amaze him how much nuance of expression Alfred could get into the barest modulation of his tone. For as long as he had known him, which had been all his life, Alfred Pennyworth had been the quintessential British butler. Elegantly formal, always proper and correct. An anachronism, a vestige of a bygone, much more refined era. He could not, under any circumstances, picture Alfred sitting with his jacket off, his shirt undone, his shoes off and his feet up, watching a football game and drinking from a can of beer. Not even in the privacy of his own room. That polished facade never cracked for an instant.

Most of the time, Alfred kept a completely neutral expression on his face that somehow managed to convey a vague sense of superiority. But at times, usually times of great stress—and Bruce Wayne's life was full of more stress than most men would ever experience, much less imagine—Alfred could display concern, anxiety, anger, sadness, the entire gamut of emotions available to any ordinary man. Yet Alfred was hardly an ordinary man. Like his father before him, Alfred Pennyworth had become what the British quaintly called "a gentleman's gentleman," but he had lived a very different life before that. He had once been a commando in the British Special Air Service, the elite SAS, and a combat medic. He could have been a doctor. He could also have been an actor, which had been his dream. He had been trained in the Royal Academy of Dramatic Arts and was a thespian of remarkable accomplishment. A gifted mimic, Alfred was able to impersonate any voice, accent, or dialect after hearing it only once, and he was a wizard with theatrical makeup. He was incredibly well read and possessed an intellect of a very high order. He could have been anything he wanted to be, but he had decided to become a butler, a mentor, and a friend to a tragically orphaned youngster named Bruce Wayne, a decision that had changed the course of his life in ways he could never have expected.

Now, in the twilight of his years, Alfred would never be anything else but what he was. And he had no desire to be anything else. Bruce had often wondered, in the past, if Alfred had felt cheated somehow, but Alfred had assured him that he found fulfillment in his duties, and in their friendship, and Bruce knew that it was true. Though to the world at large Alfred seemed no more than a servant, Bruce considered himself astonishingly lucky to have him for a friend.

It was, however, an odd friendship. Far more intimate than most, but odd just the same. In most ways, they were as close as two men could possibly be, and yet there was always that curious distance between them, like an invisible wall that just barely separated them. Cordial formality defined the limits of their relationship. It was never "Bruce," but "Mr. Wayne," or "sir," or "Master Bruce," which was as informal as Alfred ever got. Despite all his efforts, Bruce had never succeeded in getting him to drop that facade of refined dignity and formality. Alfred was, indeed, a gentleman's gentleman to the core. It was his role in life, and Alfred played it like the consummate actor that he was.

To other people, or at least to people who did not know him well, Alfred often seemed stiff, aloof and emotionless, like an automaton. The classic stereotype of the British butler. And Alfred understood the psychology of stereotypes extremely well. He could blend into the background effortlessly, like a chameleon, so that people would often forget that he was even there. Alfred knew how to use that to good advantage. Over the years, Bruce had learned to read the subtle tones and manner of his friend. Alfred could "tell" him things in a roomful of people that no one but Bruce would be able to pick up. He had a dry, ironic sense of humor that was revealed in subtle ways, in the slight lifting of an eyebrow, a barely perceptible curl to the lip, a variation in tone that would completely escape the causal listener but that would speak volumes to Bruce Wayne.

Though still extremely fit despite his advanced years, Alfred was becoming something of a curmudgeon, but this manner manifested itself in ways that were not evident to anyone but Bruce. His sense of humor, always wry and scalpel-edged, was becoming somewhat more caustic and sarcastic. Such as the remark about swinging from the rooftops on an empty stomach—amusing in itself, but the tone of delivery was ninety-nine percent of the effect.

"Very well, Alfred," he relented, "I'll have something a bit later. But right now, I just feel a need to be alone."

"Very well sir. I'll be here if you need me."

How many times over the years, Bruce wondered, had he said those words to his old friend? Certainly, more times than it was possible to count. He was a man who required a great deal of "alone time." More than most people could hope to understand. And yet, in a sense, he had *always* been alone, ever since that fateful day when two shots from a .45 caliber semiautomatic pistol had changed his life forever.

June 26th. The day of the gun. A date that was seared into his memory like an agonizing brand. June 26th. He had been eight years old and his parents, Dr. Thomas and Martha Wayne, had taken him to see *The Mark of Zorro*, starring Tyrone Power. Ironic that they had chosen that film to see. He could still remember virtually every frame and, though he possessed a videocassette of it, he never watched it. He had tried once and found it was too painful. It brought back all the memories. Memories that had never really left him, that were never very far beneath the surface.

A psychologist, if he had known all the details, might have made much of the movie's influence on him. It was the story of Don Diego De La Vega, the son of a wealthy and influential landowner in the Spanish New World colony of Los Angeles. Educated in Spain, he had returned a man, a well-rounded and well-educated man, and a champion swordsman whose body and reflexes were developed to peak condition. But the land he had returned to had changed. It had fallen under tyranny from corrupt military officials of the Spanish crown, and the people were being oppressed, abused, and taxed beyond endurance.

Diego had found himself unable to just stand by and watch the people being victimized so brutally, but he had realized early on that acting openly was not the way. If he were known to be resisting the oppression and fighting for the people, he would be a marked man and he would leave his family and those he cared for vulnerable. And so he had chosen to play the fox. He had become El Zorro, a masked and black-garbed, caped crusader fighting against injustice. As Diego, he played the part of an ineffectual fop, a rich and spoiled, indolent young man devoted to the superficial, hedonistic pleasures of the shallow life. As Zorro, he became the relentless avenger who fought against the crimes being perpetrated on the people. And his mysterious nature and ominous appearance struck terror into the hearts of his enemies.

Bruce remembered leaving the theater wishing that he could be like Zorro. It was all that he could talk about as they walked the darkened city streets. Then, in a decision that was to have fateful repercussions, his father chose to take a shortcut through an alley in an area that in years to come would become infamous as one of the most blighted and dangerous sections of the city. Crime Alley. And the crime that took place there on the night of June 26 was murder.

His name was Joe Chill. He was a nobody. A punk. A cheap hood. A gunman who placed his faith in his weapon's ability to inflict fear upon his victims. But Dr. Thomas Wayne was not afraid, and he resisted. Two shots cracked out. The first took the life of Dr. Thomas Wayne. The second felled his wife, who screamed hysterically when she saw her husband shot and launched herself at his murderer. And an eight-year-old boy named Bruce was left all alone in the world, severely traumatized, perhaps spared by the gunman named Joe Chill because he saw something in that young boy's eyes that bored into the core of him and wrenched at the paltry thing that was his soul. Something that chilled him to the bone.

Her name was Dr. Leslie Thompkins, a physician and a social worker. At night, she often walked the streets of the blighted sections of the city, searching for those who had given up on life, or thought that life had given up on them, looking to lend a helping hand because she was one of those few gentle and empathic souls who cared and who could not help but care. She found him. Crouching over the bodies of his parents, eyes staring, seeing nothing, tears coursing down his cheeks, rocking back and forth and making a low, pathetic, moaning sound. A sound that encompassed the pain of the entire world, encapsulated in an innocent young boy whose fragile reality had shattered like a fine glass sculpture, breaking into shards of razored cruelty before his very eyes.

She opened up her heart to him and took him in. She

greased the wheels of government bureaucracy and had herself appointed as his guardian, arranging things so that he could be raised at home, at Wayne Manor, because he desperately needed something familiar to hang on to, something that would keep him from spinning down into the abyss of the frightening unknown and losing himself forever. It took a lot of time, time for her to reach him, time for her to try to heal his wounds. But she had help in the form of a man named Alfred Pennyworth, who gave up his dreams of a life upon the stage to care for a boy who had seen too much of the world's cruelty at far too young an age.

For a long time, Bruce sat silent and motionless in his favorite reading chair, as he so often did, remembering.

Some wounds never heal. The time came when he found himself chafing under Leslie's guardianship. His life was good, but he had to give it meaning. And he knew just what he would do with it. He also knew that it would not be easy. He had money; his parents had been very wealthy. What he did not have were the proper tools.

He left home and embarked for Europe on an odyssey of knowledge through some of the finest universities in the world. But he was never graduated. To others, he seemed indifferent in his studies, a spoiled dilettante who appeared to take nothing very seriously. But it was then that the outward persona of Bruce Wayne was formed, the image that the world would see, though it had nothing to do with who he really was. In a sense, Bruce Wayne did not exist. He had died on that balmy summer night of June 26 in Crime Alley. The Bruce Wayne that was visible to the world was merely a facade. Behind it was another man. A man obsessed.

He took the knowledge that he needed, the knowledge that would further him upon his quest, and he moved on. He studied law and the techniques of criminology and the inner workings of the human mind. He pursued practical experience at every opportunity, apprenticing himself to a number of detectives and training his body with brutal perseverance, mastering gymnastics, techniques of meditation, boxing, and other, more esoteric forms of martial arts, pushing himself relentlessly, straining his mind and punishing his muscles with a regimen that would have sent lesser men into the hospital, always motivated by a single-minded obsession, the spark of which was born in a deserted alley on a dark night in Gotham City.

His path led him to a sanctuary in the remote mountains of Korea, where his devotion and sincerity impressed a master named Kirigi, who took him as a pupil and refined his talents and physical abilities to a point few men in the world would ever reach. With long-suffering patience and unshaking dedication, Bruce Wayne eventually became the man he had set out to be.

He returned home to Gotham City a grown man, and much changed. And yet, the force that drove him had never abated for an instant. He thought that he was ready. But he had been premature. His first endeavor at the task he had imposed upon himself was a complete disaster. He had gone to the rescue of a prostitute being beaten by her pimp, and both of them had turned on him. Then a third party had joined the fray, and he had been wounded and almost taken into custody. He barely made it home.

He remembered sitting in this very chair, feeling stunned

and shaken, wondering what had gone wrong. All those years of preparation... had it all been in vain? Had he been doomed to fail from the start? Had he fooled himself into believing that he could be something he was never meant to be? He felt adrift, confused, unfocused. If only he could figure out where he had gone wrong! If only he could somehow make sense of it all, discover what it was he had to do that he had not yet done. If only he could see some sort of sign...

And then it happened.

He got up from the chair and turned, remembering. It was that window, there. There was a thump, a crash, and something came hurtling through the window in an explosion of shattered glass. Something dark and sinister that fell to lie twitching at his feet.

A bat.

And in that moment, he had remembered. He had been a child, playing on the grounds of Wayne Manor. His parents had warned him about going near certain areas of the sprawling estate, places where the ground could be unstable. He had been running, and suddenly he was falling. He landed with a jarring impact and, for a while, he could not move. He had fallen through a hole, fallen into someplace dark, a frightening place, cold and damp, and all around him were the sounds of chittering. The chittering of bats. His fall into the cavern startled them, and they flocked all around him, their wings beating at his face, and he screamed.... He could still recall the sheer, unadulterated terror he had felt. And when his father heard his screams and came to pull him out, he remembered how he'd trembled when he asked him, "Daddy, was that Hell?"

Right there. Right there on the floor was where the bat had fallen. He remembered crouching down and bending over it. As it stared up at him with feral eyes, its twitchings grew more feeble, then they stopped. And as the creature died... something strange and inexplicable happened.

Perhaps it had only been his overwrought imagination, but for a moment, just a moment, it felt as if the bat had somehow *merged* with him. As if, in giving up its life, its soul had flown straight into him. He had felt a tightness in his chest, and then a bizarre rushing, floating sensation, a sudden sense of utter clarity and joy, an experience that zen masters call *satori,* the sudden feeling of enlightenment. And in that moment, he knew. He knew what he had been missing.

It seemed so long ago, but he could remember it all as if it had been yesterday. He left the den and went down the hall to the entrance foyer of the elegantly appointed mansion. He approached the ornate grandfather clock, a valuable antique that dated back to the Revolutionary War. The pearl-inlaid hands on the clock stood at 6:25. He opened the latch on the window of the clock face, swung it open, and changed the setting so that the hands stood at 10:47.

It was the same time indicated by the hands on his father's gold Swiss watch, that now rested in a velvet-lined case in the top drawer of the study desk. When Thomas Wayne fell to the sidewalk, victim of the killer's bullet, the crystal on the timepiece had shattered and the watch had stopped, forever marking the moment of his death. The hands on the grandfather clock reset, Bruce shut the clock-face window, then opened the long and narrow glass-fronted cover of the pull chains. He reached inside and gave one of the chains a tug. There was a soft clicking sound and the entire clock swung away from the wall, revealing a dark and narrow entryway and a flight of stairs leading down.

He had trod these stairs many times through the years, enough so that now he did not need any light, and there was something comforting about the darkness. The temperature dropped as he descended, and the humidity increased. The sound of his footsteps echoed in the narrow passageway as the wood steps gave way to steps of stone, carved into the natural rock formations that the mansion stood upon. He went down below the level of the mansion's basement and the stairway started to gradually widen. The walls on either side of him were cold, damp, rough, and unfinished stone. In the distance, he could hear a sound... the faint sound of chittering. It grew louder as he descended, but although it was a sound that had once filled him with terror, it did so no longer. It had become a friendly sound as he came to know and understand the much-maligned creatures that made it.

He reached the bottom of the stairway and stepped out into a large cavern, part of a system that honeycombed the earth beneath the bluffs on which the mansion stood. It was like entering another world. His world. Above, the palatial mansion was all shadow and no substance.

Here was where he really lived.

CHAPTER TWO

PRESSURE. Police Commissioner James Gordon was used to feeling pressure. It came with the job. Pressure from the mayor's office, pressure from the city council, pressure from citizens' groups and special-interest lobbies, and, always, pressure from the media. He often longed for the good old days when he'd been a Chicago street cop and didn't have to deal with the stress of managing a large urban police department. But even back then, things had not been exactly simple.

There was nothing simple about being a cop in a large and densely populated city. Gordon often thought that it was a job that would never get done. All the police could do, at best, was fight a holding action. Always, they were outnumbered. Always, they risked their lives in the daily performance of their duties. And always, their efforts went largely unappreciated.

Back in Chicago, Gordon had not only the rigors of

the job to deal with, but the corruption that had been rampant throughout the department. He had grown up in a time when the police officer was a figure of respect in the community, but by the time he had a shield of his own, much of that had changed. Perhaps, he thought, it came about because people had simply stopped respecting the police. Perhaps it was because the job kept growing more and more difficult, more and more hopeless, and a cynicism began to spread throughout the police departments of large cities. Perhaps it was because something had happened to the values of the country and the ideals of public service had somehow been replaced by self-seeking ambition, greed, and situational ethics. Perhaps it was a combination of all those factors. But whatever it was, things changed. The cop went from a figure of respect to a man who had his hand out.

From the least, most inoffensive-seeming freebie, such as free doughnuts and coffee at the local greasy spoon, to the bribery practiced by the numbers runners and the pimps and the pushers and the organized-crime kingpins, the cop on the pad became a universal stereotype in the big city. And the corruption often extended to the highest levels of city politics. It would have been convenient to place the blame at the feet of men who had no ethics, men who simply didn't give a damn about anybody but themselves. But once again, things were never all that simple.

What was a rookie cop to do, a fresh-faced, young idealist straight from the academy, when he was confronted with a system where all his fellow officers were on the take? How could he swim against the tide? He was new, and he was green. Making waves, waves that could get him transferred, or cashiered from the force, or even killed, was an unwise course to take. Often, he had a family to support and, often, he was grossly underpaid. And nobody seemed to give a damn about him. He was a front-line soldier in the war on crime, but the people he had sworn "to serve and protect" treated him like a pariah.

A free doughnut and a cup of coffee seemed like a perfectly harmless gratuity to accept, a show of appreciation from a local merchant, and it was no big deal. It helped save a little money. Comes the day when baby needs new shoes. Or there are doctor bills to pay. Or the apartment building just went condo and it's either fork over for a heavy mortgage or find somewhere else to live in a city where the rents keep going up. So you let a prostitute or two slide on an arrest. Why not? What's the point? Bust 'em and they're back out on the street in half an hour anyway. And it's not as if prostitution was a really serious crime, like burglary, assault, rape, or murder. Why tie up the court system with pointless prostitution busts when there are *real* criminals out there? And if the pimp gets hit for a small cut of the action, where's the harm? He makes his money from the people of the city, after all, the ones who underpay you and ignore you and treat you like a thug, and it's really no more than a sort of entertainment tax. What the hell, nobody cares and you could really use the extra money. So you take it and sell another portion of your soul.

Where do you draw the line once you have crossed over it? Hell, everybody does it, it's a fact of life, and what are you supposed to do, act like Sir Galahad and turn it down? What makes *you* so goddamn pure? What puts *you* above it all? Why should *you* be different from everybody else on the force, and from the people on the city council and in the commissioner's office and the mayor's office and the state legislature and the Congress and the White House staff and, who knows, maybe even the President himself? And then, the final damning factor, if you refuse to take the money, you're no longer one of the boys, no longer on the inside, no longer to be trusted. Who can take a stand against all that?

Jim Gordon took a stand. In Chicago, he brought down a crooked cop and it cost him his position on the force. His young wife was pregnant with their first child, there would be doctor bills to pay, and he was out of a job. He had to scramble. He found a new position as a homicide detective on the force in Gotham City, but it hadn't taken long before he found out it was the same old song. Graft. Corruption. Bribes. Half the department was on the pad. A lot of men in his position might have learned their lesson. Keep your mouth shut. Don't make waves. But Jim Gordon was an honest man, and honest men don't compromise. And there was one thing about Gotham City that was different.

Gotham City had the Batman.

The first time he appeared, Jim Gordon did not know what to make of him. A costumed vigilante, dressed up like a giant bat. The media went into full howl. At first, they thought the Batman was joke, a story with a "human interest" angle, played for laughs. Only, the Batman wasn't very funny. This was more than just some lunatic in a costume. A hell of a lot more.

Whoever the Batman was, he was no ordinary man. His talents were varied and unique, his resources considerable. And he was serious. He wasn't just some nut case looking for publicity. Quite the opposite. The TV networks and the magazines and newspapers fell all over themselves trying to get an interview with him, even going so far as to put up outrageous cash rewards. Nothing doing. Whoever the Batman was, money wasn't his priority. He created headlines by his actions, but he carefully avoided all publicity. So it was not an ego thing. That seemed to leave only one option. He was some kind of paranoid schizophrenic who'd seen too many movies and had started acting out his fantasies. And there was no shortage of psychiatrists and sociologists and other so-called "experts" in Gotham City who were only too happy to appear on television and give their hip-shot diagnoses of the Batman.

While all this was going on, the police in Gotham City didn't look too good. There was a guy running around the city dressed up like a giant bat, leaving trussed-up crooks for the police to find, and they couldn't seem to catch him. So the word went out. Bring in the Batman. "Bust his ass," said the commissioner, "and get him off the streets before the whole city starts to think we're nothing but a bunch of fools." But, once again, things weren't all that simple. There was a hidden agenda.

The Batman was having an effect. Of what use were bribes if they could not protect the criminals of Gotham City from some "caped crusader" who came at them from the shadows? The extra income of officers on the pad started to fall off. Worse than that, they found out that the Batman was after *them* as well. The word went out through other channels. If we can't arrest this weirdo, *waste* him. Only, that was easier said than done.

Jim Gordon knew exactly what it meant to have the word go out on you. It had gone out on him. Shortly after he became a cop in Gotham City, the word went out that Jim Gordon wasn't to be trusted. He didn't take money, and you can't trust a cop who won't take money. The other cops started to regard him with suspicion. Not all of them. There were many good cops on the force. Good cops who took money. Not because they wanted to, but because they felt they had no choice. It was hard to buck the system, and the system was corrupt. A lot of them admired Gordon and respected him, but they kept their distance. They didn't want to be around when he went down.

The word was out that Jim Gordon was not only a cop who couldn't be bought, but he was also a whistleblower, like Frank Serpico in New York City. Everybody knew what happened to Frank Serpico. So Jim Gordon found himself in the unusual position of being one of the two men marked by the corrupt element in the police department as serious trouble. The other man was a man he had been ordered to bring in.

At first, Gordon had no problem with that. His main problem concerned the corrupt officials in the department, the ones who tainted everybody else, and he was busy gathering evidence against them, watching his back at the same time. The Batman was a vigilante who took the law into his own hands. Gordon had no conflict with being ordered to bring him in. But, yet again, things weren't all that simple.

Just how far did the Batman go with "taking the law into his own hands"? There was no law against wearing a costume. A citizen was entitled to free expression. There was no law against concealing one's identity, so long as it was not concealed for criminal purposes. A citizen was entitled to privacy and anonymity if he or she so chose.

There was no law against patrolling the city streets, so long as a citizen did not misrepresent himself as a police officer or carry lethal weapons. Neighborhood Watch committees and citizen's protective associations did it all the time. And a citizen had the power of making a citizen's arrest, as defined in the legal code. It was essentially the same legal power of arrest given to private security agencies and detectives. When it came right down to it, Gordon thought, the Batman wasn't really breaking any laws.

He did not carry any lethal weapons. He had some fascinating gadgets, but no one could testify to ever having seen him with a gun. He did not, so far as anybody knew, ever represent himself as an officer of the law. He had interfered with crimes being committed, but he had never formally made an arrest. He had left the perpetrators tied up for the police, or knocked unconscious, but in every case, a good lawyer could easily justify his actions under the legal powers of citizen's arrest. He concealed his identity, but again, so far as anybody knew, he did not do so for purposes of fraud or for the commission of any other type of crime. However, a large gray area existed there.

If the department was determined to find sufficient cause to bring someone up on charges, they could usually find something. It might not hold up in court, but it could at least provide a basis for arrest. In the Batman's case, the department had no difficulty finding grounds on which to order him brought in. Assault, for one thing. The Batman would not cooperate with cops who sought to question him or bring him in, so that was resisting a police officer, and resisting arrest, and fleeing a warrant, and interference with a police investigation. The department had no difficulty finding grounds on which to bring charges against the Batman. They were perfectly sound and reasonable charges, too. Jim Gordon had no conflict there. The conflict came later, when Gordon finally had his first encounter with the Batman.

It began innocently enough. A runaway truck. A homeless woman in its path. Gordon could not stop the truck in time, but out of nowhere, *he* was there, shoving the old woman out of the vehicle's way at the last instant. Gordon's partner got the drop on him and radioed for backup, but the Batman slipped away and took shelter inside an abandoned building. And that was when everything went crazy.

They brought in a SWAT team. They brought in helicopters. They brought in a fleet of cruisers. They went after him with everything they had, as if some group of well-armed terrorists were holed up in that ruined building. Gordon stood outside and watched as World War III broke out in there. There were dozens of machine guns firing at shadows, tear-gas canisters exploding, they had even bombed the goddamn building, yet still the Batman got away without seriously injuring a single officer. What was even more astonishing, he eluded capture by somehow summoning a huge flock of bats to confuse his pursuers. It was like something out of a science-fiction movie. Jim Gordon had no idea how he did it, or what to make of it, but he was left with two distinct impressions. One, the Batman was *definitely* not an ordinary man. And two, the department had overreacted insanely. Property had been damaged, fires had been started, and innocent bystanders could easily have been killed. For what? The Batman had saved the life of a hapless old woman and, in return, the department had tried everything short of nuking him. Jim Gordon began to feel conflicted.

What tore it was the kidnapping of his infant son. It was done on the orders of "The Roman," Gotham City's biggest crime boss, but Gordon knew The Roman wasn't interested in ransom from a street cop. Gordon was getting too close to exposing the ties between certain high city officials and the organized crime elements in Gotham City. The Roman had his own ways of looking out for his best interests. The Batman had saved Jim Gordon's child, and his intervention allowed Gordon to arrest the kidnapper, who sang like a canary. It had exposed the biggest scandal since the Knapp Commission cleaned house in New York City. A new administration was brought in, and Gordon was promoted to captain. He had the Batman to thank for that promotion, and for the life of his infant son as well.

However, the new administration was just as anxious to get the Batman off the streets as the old, corrupt administration was. To them, the Batman was a public menace, an outlaw vigilante. So the word went out again. Arrest him. Get him off the streets. Only, things had changed considerably since the Batman first appeared.

Once the media stopped regarding the Batman as a joke, which hadn't taken very long, they had taken up the hue and cry to get him off the streets. At least, that was what they did until they discovered that a significant percentage of the people in the city, a very *large* percentage, liked the Batman and supported him. To many people the Batman was a hero, and they didn't like it when the media tried to portray him as a criminal. The media learned something else, as well. Since the Batman first appeared, the crime statistics had gone down. And they discovered that while the city and police administrations were out to get the Batman, the rank-and-file street cops took a very different view.

Not one of them could be persuaded to speak his or her mind on camera or on tape. But off camera, and strictly off the record, a lot of them said things like, "All right, if you go strictly by the book, he breaks the law, but as far as I'm concerned, the Batman's on *our* side. You ask me, he's one of the good guys. A citizen who gives a damn. He wants to run around dressed up like a bat, that's his business, but let me clue you in—it *works*. With the Batman on the streets, the crime rate's gone way down. The day he starts packin' a piece and shooting people, okay, I'll be the first one out there trying to bring him in. But until that day, I ain't gonna bust my chops, know what I mean?"

Jim Gordon was one of those who was not about to bust his chops to bring the Batman in. He owed him, for the life of his infant son and for a lot of other things as well. In the years since Gordon first arrived in Gotham City, a lot of things had changed. The police force was no longer corrupt, in part thanks to the Batman. The crooked cop was now the exception, not the rule. And Jim Gordon, once a cop regarded as a troublemaker because he would not go on the pad, was now commissioner of police. It sounded like a happy ending, but again, things were never quite that simple.

Pressure. By now, Gordon was used to feeling pressure. It was the kind of thing a man with backbone could get used to, but it was *never* easy. Some things never change. The mayor still wanted the Batman off the streets. The governor wasn't nuts about him, either. Most of the city council took a dim view of the Batman, as did some members of the Chamber of Commerce. He wasn't good for the city's image, they said. He makes it look as if the mayor's office, the city council and the police can't do their job without the help of some flamboyant vigilante. He sets a bad example. What would happen if other citizens took it in their heads to get involved the way he did? What do you think we'd have? "I don't know," Gordon often felt like saying, "law and order?" Only, he didn't say that. At least, not out loud.

Pressure. The pressure of wondering what would happen if these people learned that instead of trying to bring the Batman in, he was actively working with him. The pressure of wondering how they would react if they discovered that the Batman had become his friend. And the pressure of wondering what would happen to the city if something were to happen to his friend. A friend whose true identity he didn't even know.

He had once tried to find out who the Batman really was. He even had a list of suspects. Given his resources, the Batman had to be either a wealthy man himself or have someone with serious bucks behind him. He had to be someone reasonably young and very fit. Someone with a high order of intelligence and quick instincts under pressure. At one time, Gordon had suspected that Bruce Wayne could be the Batman.

Wayne was young and fit and fabulously wealthy. He had parlayed the money that his father left him into one of the largest fortunes in the country. But he stopped suspecting Wayne after he had met him. A less likely candidate to be the Batman he could not imagine. Wayne was a dissipated playboy, with no concern for anything except his own pleasure and amusement. Well, that was not entirely true. He did contribute to a lot of charities, and he had organized the Wayne Foundation, but then, he'd doubtless done it for purposes of tax relief. No, Bruce Wayne couldn't be the Batman. He was basically likable and charming, but he was also shallow and superficial and he did not strike Gordon as being particularly bright. With his money, he could hire others to manage his vast fortune and do his thinking for him.

Another suspect Gordon had considered at one time was David Jacks, the investment banking tycoon who owned some of the most valuable commercial property in Gotham City. Jacks was about the right age, and he seemed very fit. He was sharp, too, smart and highly competitive. Gordon had not been the only one to speculate that Jacks might be the Batman. Nor did Jacks deny it; the idea seemed to amuse him. But that had not panned out. Gordon could account for a number of instances in which the Batman and Jacks had been seen in different places at the same time. Several of those times, Gordon had been with the Batman himself.

He had considered several other candidates, but in each and every case, as with Jacks and Wayne, their whereabouts could be accounted for in one way or another during times when the Batman had been seen. He finally gave it up and decided he'd be better off not knowing who the Batman really was. That knowledge could be a liability to both of them. The important thing was that Gordon knew *what* the Batman was. He was an honest man in many ways, a man not unlike himself. A man who would not compromise his ethics or his beliefs.

He was a friend to the honest people of the city, a friend to the police, and a sworn enemy to all those who would oppose them. He was a man who cared enough to put his own life on the line in the name of justice, and a man who would not kill regardless of the provocation or the circumstances. In short, a hero. Corny? Maybe. Jim Gordon didn't think so. However, there were a lot of important people, people who could bring pressure to bear, who didn't think the same way he did. One of them was a man named Reese Chambers.

"Your people are falling down on the job, Commissioner," Chambers said as he entered Gordon's office without knocking.

"I didn't hear you knock, Mr. Chambers," Gordon said in a level tone as he looked up at him from his desk.

Chambers put his hands on the edge of the desk and leaned forward slightly toward Gordon. "Look, let's get something straight, Commissioner," he said. "Around here, your people might jump every time you snap your fingers, but I'm *not* one of your people."

"That's fortunate for you," said Gordon softly.

Chambers met his gaze. "You have something against the Bureau, Commissioner?"

"No Mr. Chambers, I have nothing against the FBI. It's you that I don't particularly care for."

"I see," said Chambers stiffly, straightening up. "All right. Maybe we should clear the air. If you've got something personal against me, Commissioner, I'd like to hear it."

"You have a fine record with the Bureau, Chambers," Gordon said. "I know. I checked. But your manner leaves a lot to be desired. Ever since you got here, you've been throwing your weight around and acting as if the Gotham City police are a bunch of cub scouts next to the FBI. That's not a good way to win friends and influence people. Especially people you're going to have to work with."

Chambers took a deep breath and let it out slowly. He nodded. "All right, Commissioner. Your point's well taken."

"Is it?"

"Yes, sir, it is. I've been under a great deal of stress, Commissioner. If I've been a bit peremptory with your people, I apologize. But I've got a tough job to do and about a hundred people breathing down my neck, trying to tell me how to do it. If I've stepped on any toes, I'm sorry, but I haven't had a lot of time to think about observing all the niceties."

"I appreciate your position, Mr. Chambers," Gordon said. "And the apology, as well. Why don't we try beginning this conversation from scratch? Have a seat."

He beckoned Chambers to a chair, and the FBI man sat.

"Can I offer you a cup of coffee?" Gordon asked.

"Yes, thanks, I could use it," Chambers said. "I've been on my feet for almost forty-eight hours straight."

Gordon picked up his phone and punched a button. "Sergeant Capiletti, would you be so kind as to bring in a couple of cups of coffee?" He glanced up at Chambers and raised his eyebrows.

"Black, please," said Chambers.

"One black, one black with sugar," Gordon said. "Thank you." He hung up the phone. "Now then, what's this about my people falling down on the job?"

"It's about this Batman character," said Chambers.

"What about him?"

"I don't like the idea of him running around loose while we've got this situation with Garcia," Chambers said. "Your people can't seem to bring him in. Not only that, but I get the distinct impression that they're not particularly anxious to try."

"You've got nothing to worry about from the Batman, Chambers," Gordon said.

"Is that right? What makes you so sure?"

There was a knock at the door, and the sergeant came in with the coffee.

"Thank you, Sergeant," Gordon said. "Oh, Capiletti, before you go..."

"Sir?"

"Agent Chambers seems to think the Batman poses some sort of security risk to his operation here. Perhaps you'd care to give him your opinion?"

"The Batman?" Capiletti said. He glanced at Chambers. "You're barkin' up the wrong tree, Mr. Chambers."

"What makes you think so, Sergeant?" Chambers asked.

"You ever met the Batman, sir?" asked Capiletti.

Chambers grimaced wryly. "No, I don't believe I've had that pleasure," he replied sarcastically.

"Well, I have."

Chambers frowned. "You've actually *met* him? Spoken with him?"

"Yes, sir, I have. Back when I was a rookie workin' the streets. He saved my life. It's a long story, so I won't bore you with it, but if the Bureau's worried about the Batman, then they're worried over nothing'. The Batman's okay in my book."

"Because he saved your life," said Chambers.

"That's part of it," admitted Capiletti, "but it's not all of it. Not by a long shot. You're not from Gotham City, sir, so of course you wouldn't know, but there are a lot of people in this town, cops and citizens alike, who think the Batman's doing one hell of a job."

"Thank you, Sergeant," Gordon said. "That will be all."

"Sir," said Capiletti.

"That's precisely the sort of attitude I'm talking about," said Chambers after Capiletti left. "This bizarre vigilante seems to have captured the imagination of a lot of people in this city, *including* the police. Frankly, I don't find that very reassuring. The man's a criminal, and he strikes me as being dangerous and unpredictable."

"That's where you're wrong, Chambers," Gordon said. "The Batman is nothing if not predictable. He'll be out there on the streets tonight, as he is most every night, and the only people he'll be posing a danger to are felons. General Garcia might be the most celebrated felon we have in Gotham City at the moment, but he's already in custody. The Batman doesn't concern himself with felons who are already in custody. It's the ones running around loose who need to worry."

"You sound as if you actually approve of him," said Chambers with disbelief.

"What I approve or disapprove of is not the issue," Gordon replied. "I'm just giving you the facts. Even if the Batman took it in his head to do anything about General Garcia, and I can't imagine why he would, what do you expect him to do? Break into the Gotham City jail and get at Garcia in maximum security?"

"Garcia's not my only concern," said Chambers.

"Oh, I see," said Gordon. "You're worried about your witness."

"That's right," said Chambers. "There are people who'd pay an awful lot of money to have that witness taken out of the picture."

Gordon chuckled.

"What's so funny?"

"Oh, I'm not laughing at you, Chambers," Gordon said. "Merely at the implied suggestion that the Batman might undertake a contract."

"You think that's laughable? We're talking about some very powerful people here, Commissioner. People with access to one hell of a lot of money."

"I have no doubt of that," said Gordon. "But rest assured, money cannot buy the Batman."

"You seem awful sure of that."

"I'm absolutely certain of it," Gordon said. "The Batman can't be bought, and you can take that to the bank. The Batman's not a killer. He's never taken a life. He doesn't even carry any lethal weapons."

"A *nonviolent* vigilante?" Chambers said.

"I didn't say he was nonviolent," Gordon replied. "I said he's never taken a life."

"There's always a first time."

Gordon shook his head. "Not in this case. If there's one thing I know about the Batman, it's that he reveres human life. It's part of what makes him tick. He also believes in justice. That's one of the reasons why he enjoys so much support in Gotham City. He's not a killer. it goes against everything he seems to believe in."

"So what are you telling me, that he's got some kind of Wyatt Earp complex?" Chambers said, frowning.

"Wyatt Earp had no compunctions about killing," Gordon replied. "The Batman won't even carry a gun. Maybe that's why he's captured the imagination of the people in this city, as you put it. If he *did* carry a gun, every single cop in this department would be out there doing everything he could to bring him in. Myself included. And most of the citizens of Gotham City would support us one hundred percent. But you see, that's what makes the Batman different and unique. He knows that if he were to use lethal force, he'd be putting himself on the same level with the criminals he hates. And that's something he would never do."

"I'd like to be as certain of that as you seem to be, Commissioner," said Chambers. "I really would. It would mean one less thing for me to worry about, and I've already got more than my share of worries."

"The Batman isn't one of them," Gordon said. "Trust me."

"You actually admire him, don't you?" Chambers said with surprise.

"In a way, I suppose I do," Gordon admitted, "although if you quote me on that, I'll deny it."

Chambers smiled. "Your secret's safe with me, Commissioner. But tell me something, don't you think it's a little weird, a grown man dressed up like a bat out there patrolling the streets at night?"

"That's exactly what I thought at first," said Gordon. "I'm not sure why he chose the image that he did, but the funny thing is that it works. Actually, it's not really all that funny. There are some highly respected psychologists who think his reasoning is very sound, regardless of his motivations. Put yourself in the criminal's place. A lot of criminals are highly superstitious to begin with. The effect of a powerful image is something they all understand, even if only subconsciously. The bat is a creature of the darkness. So is the criminal, by and large, but the bat's radar allows it to 'see' in the dark, so it's completely in its element. And there's something sinister in its appearance. In actual fact, the bat is a perfectly harmless creature, but people have always been frightened of it. It's always been associated with the supernatural, with things like vampires and such. To you and me, sitting here and drinking coffee in this brightly lit office, the idea of a grown man dressed up like a bat might seem amusing, 'a little weird,' as you put it. But if we were all alone here at night and the lights were out, and the Batman suddenly appeared right here in this office, I'd lay odds that at the very least, you'd be considerably startled. Perhaps even frightened.''

"So you're saying he does it because it gives him a psychological edge?" said Chambers. He nodded. "Interesting concept. Assuming he's worked it out that way himself. But suppose he's just a nut case?"

"I considered that as well," said Gordon. "But the evidence doesn't support that theory. The evidence is that what he does, he does in a very reasoned, rational, and calculated manner."

"That could describe a sociopath as well," said Chambers.

"True," Gordon replied, "but the Batman's not a sociopath. A sociopath is incapable of feeling empathy, and that does not describe the Batman. People who've encountered him, especially people whom he's helped, all testify to the fact that he appears to be a very caring individual. His primary motivation seems to be a deep concern for justice. A sociopath would not fit that description."

Chambers nodded. "Okay. I'll accept that. For the time being, at least. Though I'd still feel a hell of a lot better if he was off the streets. I've got enough on my hands as it is without having to worry about any wild cards."

"This isn't just routine caution, is it?" Gordon said. "Something's happened. What?"

Chambers exhaled heavily. "I'm not really sure. We've heard some rumors. At this point, we're just trying to cover all the bases. We've been keeping certain key individuals under surveillance, and one of them has started acting a bit strange lately."

"You're not going to tell me who?" asked Gordon.

Chambers shook his head. "It's not that I don't trust you, Commissioner. Honest. It's just that in this case, what you don't know can't hurt you. It's a somewhat delicate situation, politically speaking. There could be adverse repercussions."

"Is there anything I can do to help?" asked Gordon.

Chambers shook his head. "Not at the moment, no." He shrugged. "And maybe it's nothing. Maybe we're all getting a little paranoid. But I'll tell you one thing, I'll be happy when the trial finally gets under way and it's all over. We're all getting a bit edgy, and Garcia's lawyers aren't making matters any easier." He sighed and got up. "Sorry to have taken up your time, Commissioner."

"It's no trouble," Gordon said. "Always happy to cooperate with the Bureau."

"And we appreciate it," Chambers said. He paused. "What happens if you do manage to arrest him?"

"You mean the Batman?" Gordon said. He smiled. "I don't know. But it would sure be interesting."

Chambers grinned. "You know, in a way I sort of envy him," he said.

"Really? How's that?" asked Gordon.

"He doesn't have to deal with lawyers and bureaucrats and federal witnesses," Chambers said wryly.

"I hear that," said Gordon, smiling.

"I'll remember what you said and try to walk a little softer," Chambers said. "What the hell, we're all in this together, aren't we? Thanks for the coffee."

"Anytime," said Gordon. Perhaps he'd been a little harsh in his initial judgement of Chambers, he thought as he sipped his coffee. The man was under a lot of pressure. There seemed to be a lot of that going around lately. It came with the territory. Chambers wasn't the only one who'd be relieved when this thing with Garcia was over and done with. The government was doing everything in its power to expedite the scheduling of the trial. The lawyers would do everything they could to drag it out, but Garcia would undoubtedly be convicted and shipped off to federal prison. Naturally, there would be appeals and the whole process would drag on in the courts for years, but at least that wouldn't be his headache. By then, the pressure would be off. It would be nice to get back to business as usual.

"That's a lovely dress," said the ambassador. "Is it a designer original?"

Her smile was dazzling. "Believe it or not, I made it myself from a pattern in a magazine," she replied with a wink.

She did, indeed, make it easy for him. Their eyes met repeatedly during the reception. She knew how to work a room, and she seemed to captivate everyone she spoke to, but she kept coming back to him. When they left together, she had slipped her arm through his as if it was the most natural thing in the world. They drove back to his apartment, and she leaned against him as they left the car and went inside. In the lobby, as they waited for the elevator, she kissed him, and it was electric. They continued kissing in the elevator on the way up, but the moment they entered his apartment, her entire manner changed.

She put her finger to his lips, then whispered in his ear, "Make only casual small talk. Ask me if I'd like a drink."

He frowned, faintly puzzled, and did as she requested. She asked him for a scotch on the rocks, with a dash of soda. As he went to the bar to make the drinks, she walked around the apartment, commenting on his good taste and making small talk, but in her hand she carried a small electronic box she'd taken from her purse. To his astonishment, she found several concealed microphones. One on his telephone, one underneath the coffee table by the couch, one in the bedroom, one in the kitchen, and one in the bathroom. He couldn't believe it. They'd bugged his whole apartment!

She left the bugs where they were, took out a small pad of paper, and wrote him a note. "Get the money."

"I'll be right back," he told her. "Make yourself comfortable."

He went into the bedroom and opened a safe behind a concealed panel in the closet. He suddenly felt overwhelmed with apprehension. The safe had been installed by embassy workers, but the Americans had him under surveillance. It couldn't be anybody else. Could they have found it? Did they know about the money? He didn't think so, but he couldn't be sure. He had only brought it into the apartment late that afternoon. His people had assured him that it could not be traced, but he was no longer sure of anything. How long had he been under surveillance? He desperately tried to think if he might have said anything in the apartment, or over the telephone, that could implicate him. Damn it, why did he have to be the one entrusted with this?

He brought the case out into the living room. She opened it, glanced quickly at the money, beckoned him to the couch, and started taking it out of the case. "Mmm, darling," she said as she started to tuck the packets of bills into cleverly concealed pockets sewn on the inside of her coat. He realized that whoever was listening would think that they were making love. When she was done, she sat back down and finished her drink. He did not know what to say.

She smiled and kissed him on the lips. "Why don't we go into the bedroom?" she said.

CHAPTER
THREE

"THERE she is," said Agent Palmer, watching the entrance of the building. He took several high-speed photographs of the woman leaving, then checked his watch and grimaced. "Four hours. Looks like the ambassador had himself a nice time. Do we follow her or sit tight?"

Jernigan watched the woman get into the ambassador's car. "I doubt he's going anywhere tonight. And if he does, or if he makes any calls, we'll know about it. It's probably nothing, but it can't hurt to check her out."

Palmer put down the camera and turned the key in the ignition. He pulled away from the curb, following the ambassador's car at a discreet distance. It was late and traffic was light, so he stayed well back. They followed the car to the Gotham Plaza hotel and watched her get out and go into the lobby.

"Well, whoever she is, she goes first class," said

Jernigan. "Let's give her a few minutes to get to her room, then go find out from the desk clerk who she is."

However, no sooner had the ambassador's car pulled away than she was coming out of the hotel again.

"Wait a minute," Jernigan said. "What's going on here?"

The doorman got a cab for her and she got inside.

"That's interesting," said Palmer as he turned to follow the cab. "I think maybe we've got something here."

They followed the cab into a neighborhood that was anything but prime real estate, down by the waterfront docks and the sex bars. The cab pulled over to the curb and the woman got out, paid the driver, and started walking.

"Strange place for a woman to come at this hour of the night," Palmer said.

"Especially alone," Jernigan added. They watched her cross the street and head toward the deserted, shadowed area underneath the elevated highway.

"Keep well back," Jernigan said. "We don't want her to spot us."

"Can you see her?" asked Palmer, pulling over and squinting through the windshield.

"Hang on a minute," Jernigan replied, picking up a pair of night glasses. He looked through them. "Yeah. She's just standing there, underneath the highway."

"She's gotta be meeting someone," said Palmer.

"That's what I figure," Jernigan replied, watching through the binoculars. "If you ask me, in this area she's taking one hell of a chan—" The rear window shattered suddenly and Jernigan pitched forward against the dash as the bullet smashed through the back of his head and blew out the front of his skull. Blood and brains and bone fragments splattered the inside of the windshield.

"Jesus!" shouted Palmer, but he got no further. The second shot came immediately on the heels of the first, from a silenced, high-powered semiautomatic, and the impact threw him against the wheel.

The woman standing in the shadows underneath the highway heard a car horn go off. The sound kept blaring through the night until, a moment or two later, it was suddenly cut off. She looked around nervously and bit her lower lip. She opened her purse and put her hand on the butt of the snub-nosed .38 caliber revolver she kept in there. Its presence reassured her slightly, but only slightly.

Damn it, she thought, I don't *need* this. The thought of being in this neighborhood alone, with all that money in her coat, and the incredible chances she was taking . . . But for a hundred thousand dollars, tax free, it was worth it. Not that she'd had much choice. She was in too deep. They had too much on her. It would have been tempting to simply take off with the million, except she didn't think she'd get too far. And even if she did, she had no desire to spend the rest of her life looking over her shoulder. No, she thought, this would be the last time. She'd turn over the money, take her hundred grand, hop the first plane to the Cayman Islands, clean out her numbered account, and disappear somewhere in Argentina, Mexico, or Costa Rica, where the money she had squirreled away selling information could buy her a very comfortable lifestyle.

She heard the sound of wheels crunching on gravel and quickly turned around, the .38 Special in her hand. The black Mercedes pulled up to her slowly. She raised her hand, shielding her eyes from the glare of the headlights. The car pulled even with her and the driver rolled the window down.

"You've brought the money?" he said, speaking with a Continental accent.

"It's in the coat you gave me, just the way you said," she replied.

"Excellent. Get in."

She put the gun back inside her purse and went around the front of the car to get in on the passenger side. She shut the door as she got in. A moment later, there was a soft, chuffing sound and the car door opened once again. Her body came tumbling out. She was no longer wearing the coat. The black Mercedes drove away into the night.

Kiyotero Sato awoke at four A.M., as he always did, without benefit of an alarm clock. He did not sleep in a bed, but on a woven tatami mat, with a small wood block for a pillow. His home, such as it was, consisted of a small corner of a rented loft above a Szechuan restaurant. At one time, when "gentrification" had overflowed Gotham Village and started reaching into Chinatown, some of the old lofts had been renovated and refurbished, converted into fashionable residences with refinished wood floors, modern bathrooms, and kitchens with built-in appliances and track lighting. But the yuppies had not succeeded in taking over Chinatown, so they had moved on to greener pastures in neighborhoods like Coventry and Manchester. Chinatown continued on pretty much the way it always was, a small slice of another world, an alien culture in the heart of Gotham City.

The loft that Sato rented from the owners of the building had been one of those renovated by some member of the artsy set. It had a beautifully finished wood floor and the walls had been left in the rough brick, all except one, which ran the length of the loft and was finished in rich, dark mahogany paneling. The skylights had been left in place; the loft's designer had opted for atmosphere instead of a dropped ceiling, and access to the loft was through a large freight elevator from the ground floor.

Sato had done little to the premises since he moved in. The loft was ideal for his purposes, and the price was right. The owners of the building, who also owned and operated the restaurant downstairs, had let him have it very cheaply, both out of respect for a man of his position in the community and because he had agreed to instruct their children and the staff of their restaurant in the martial arts.

Except for the small, screened-off corner where he slept, the loft had been turned into a dojo. On the wood-paneled wall hung an American flag and, beside it, separated from it by a large, framed painting of Bodhidharma, hung a Japanese flag. An assortment of weapons hung upon the wall in orderly rows. There were bokans, sai, nunchaku, katanas, kama, spears, shuriken, and various other esoteric weapons of the martial arts. Kendo armor and padded canvas helmets with steel face guards were stacked in orderly fashion against the wall. Sato used them not only to instruct his students in the art of kendo, but to facilitate safe full-contact sparring. He eschewed the Western innovation of foam-rubber gloves and boots. It was possible to be severely injured with such "safeguards," while wearing some forty pounds of kendo armor and lightly padded speedbag gloves not only provided a greater measure of protection, but increased one's fighting abilities as well.

Sato rolled to his feet gracefully, with a suppleness that belied his age. No one knew exactly how old he was, and he did not volunteer the information. He did not volunteer anything at all about his past. What was known about him by his students and by the people of the community was sketchy, at best. He was an Okinawan who had lived in China. That much was known. There were rumors, but it was impossible to substantiate any of them. Some claimed that he was once a high official in one tong or another, or that he had fought for the Japanese during the war and had been among the very last to surrender, that he had been found years after the war was over on some remote Pacific island, or that he was a Buddhist monk who had fallen afoul of the communist Chinese. But all that was no more than speculation, and Sensei Sato, as he was known in the community, did not feel the need to enlighten anyone about his history.

There was really only one thing that anyone needed to know about him, one thing that mattered. He was a master. Of what rank, nobody knew, as Sato never wore a colored belt. Nor did he award them. Black belts, brown belts, yellow, red and blue belts of various degrees, all meant nothing to Sato. "The purpose of a belt," he often said, "is to hold up one's trousers."

His somewhat nontraditional approach to martial arts had caused some of the other so-called masters in the city to repudiate him, and not a few of them had come to attend his classes so that they could test his skill. The moment he perceived their intentions, Sato invited them to leave. Unlike many others, he did not choose to call himself a master. He preferred the simple title "Sensei." Teacher. He had no interest in proving anything to anyone. Nor did he encourage this practice in his students. He would not allow them to enter tournaments. "They are called the martial arts," he always said whenever someone asked why, "and not the martial sports. If you have a desire to compete, play basketball."

He did not keep pine boards on hand, because he saw no purpose in breaking boards. "In all my life," he said, "I have never heard of anyone attacked by a board." Once, upon examining the built-up knuckles of a student who had won black belts in several styles, Sato had remarked, "These are not the hands of a gentleman. If you wish to break bricks, I suggest you use a sledgehammer. It is much more efficient." When asked if it was not necessary to toughen up the hands and feet for combat, Sato would reply, "It requires a mere three pounds of force to break the human knee. If you wish to break the knees of elephants, I cannot help you. I am fond of elephants."

A new student once asked Sato how long it would take to earn a black belt. Sato had promptly given him one. "There," he told the student. "You now possess a black belt. If that satisfies you, then you have saved the cost of your tuition."

The student hadn't understood. He said he meant to ask how long it would take for him to acquire the knowledge that would *entitle* him to wear the belt. "Do you measure knowledge by the color of your socks?"

asked Sato. "The worth of knowledge is intrinsic in itself. Seek knowledge for its own sake, not for the sake of showing others how much you have acquired. I cannot measure the worth of your knowledge. You must do that for yourself."

Some of Sato's students had asked him when they could start learning to use some of the weapons on the wall. "When you are ready," he replied. But he never told any of them they were ready. It took the brightest of them over a year to figure it out. One day, he simply approached Sato and said, "Sensei, I am ready to learn the bokan." And Sato had taken one down and started to instruct him in its use.

Some of Sato's students had once asked him about the teaching of philosophy. He told them to watch Oprah Winfrey. They were somewhat taken aback, but they complied. Several weeks later, they came back to report that they could not understand what her philosophy was. "Neither can I," admitted Sato with a perfectly straight face.

Sato's school did not have a name. It was not listed in the phone book, because he did not have a phone. His students wore no patches, because he did not sell them any and he did not teach any particular style. He was skilled in various techniques of karate, tai kwan do, hapkido, kung fu, judo, aikido, hua rang do, kendo, and ninjitsu, and he taught a mixture of them all. When asked which style was the best, he always said, "The one that works."

Sato's idiosyncratic manner confused many students, and those who came to him with any preconceptions or particular expectations usually did not last very long unless they were able to adapt. The ones that lasted soon found their personalities beginning to undergo a change. Invariably, they became more mellow and laid back. They found that things troubled them a great deal less. They slept better and they needed less sleep. They found their energy increasing. Even the dullest of them soon developed a wry sense of humor, and they began to take satisfaction in ordinary, everyday aspects of their lives. And they became absolutely lethal. There was a strong camaraderie among them, and they were like family to one another. All save one. And that one was not a student. Not exactly.

Sato knew the instant he arrived. From behind the partition, he called out, "Good morning. May I offer you a cup of tea?"

The Batman smiled. He'd been certain that he hadn't made the slightest sound when he came down through the skylight. It had become almost a ritual with them. Each time, he tried to take Sato by surprise with his arrival. And every time, he failed.

"Thank you, Sensei," he called out from the center of the dojo. "I would like some tea."

Sato came out carrying a lacquered tray bearing a small pot of tea and two delicate china cups. The Batman gave him a respectful bow. Sato inclined his head slightly in response. He set the tray down on a low table near the wall and kneeled down on a tatami mat. He beckoned the Batman to join him.

"What gave me away this time?" the Batman asked.

"Everything," said Sato. "You move like an ox."

"That bad?"

"Well, a subtle ox," conceded Sato.

The Batman grinned. "Then I must be improving."

Sato grunted and poured him a cup of tea.

"*Domo arrigato,*" said the Batman in flawless Japanese.

"*De nada,*" replied Sato incongruously, in Spanish. "So, the city has been rendered safe for one more day?"

"It's been an uneventful night," replied the Batman, ignoring the gentle sarcasm.

"No night is ever uneventful," Sato said.

"I stand corrected. I mean that it's been an uneventful night for me."

"And this displeases you?"

"Only in the sense that if any crime took place tonight, I was not in the right place to prevent it."

"Ah," said Sato, "Then tonight has been a disappointment for you."

"Not entirely," said Batman. "I know I can't be everywhere at once, but I like to think my presence out there has at least some deterrent effect. Besides, I like the night. I find it comforting. And any night when I can visit you is never a disappointment."

Sato gave him a slight smile. "I, too, look forward to your visits. You never cease to interest me."

"And yet you've never once asked me who I am."

"You are the Masked Rodent," Sato said.

"I'm serious," said Batman.

"You are *not* the Masked Rodent?" said Sato, raising his eyebrows in pretended shock.

"Getting a straight answer out of you is like trying to squeeze blood out of stone," said the Batman. There were times when Sato's peculiar sense of humor could be trying. He never referred to him as the Batman but always insisted on calling him the Masked Rodent. It irritated him, which was why Sato did it.

Sato put down his teacup. "Very well," he said. "I will give only straight answers tonight. What do you wish to know?"

"You've never asked me anything about myself. You've never tried to follow me, or find out who I am, or how I found you, or where I'd studied. I've often wondered why."

"If I had asked, would you have told me?"

"No."

Sato shrugged. "So what would be the point?"

"But you're not even curious?"

"I did not say that. If you had wished to reveal those things to me, you would have done so. That you do not wish to reveal them does not concern me. Your reasons are your own, and I respect them."

"I'm grateful for that, Sensei," said the Batman. "And for your agreeing to see me under such unusual circumstances."

"It is not entirely unselfish on my part," admitted Sato. "It has been many years since I have known anyone whose skill equaled my own. And, as I have said, you interest me."

"I wish I was free to satisfy your curiosity," said Batman.

"But you do," Sato replied. "Each time you come, I discover more about you. Each time we speak, you reveal more about yourself. Not only from the things you say, but from the things you do not say. And the way in which you do not say them."

"Now I'm curious," the Batman said, drinking his tea. "What have you learned?"

"Much," said Sato. "I have learned that you are a deeply disturbed person."

"Thanks a lot," the Batman said wryly.

"I did not mean that I think you are unbalanced, though it would not be difficult to present an argument for that," said Sato. "However, there are things that cause you much distress. At some time in your life, you have experienced great pain. A devastating personal loss, which you have never quite recovered from. One could theorize that this loss concerned a woman—a wife, perhaps, or a woman who was not your wife, but whom you cared for deeply. And yet, it is clear that the nature of this loss was instrumental in the formation of your character, so it must have occurred when you were very young. I suspect that it concerned your parents, that perhaps they died as a result of some criminal act. Possibly you were present when they died. It affected you profoundly, so much so that you resolved to devote your life to fighting crime. Your family was very wealthy, or perhaps you amassed great wealth yourself as you grew older, but the accumulation of this wealth was always directed toward a single purpose. The one main purpose that motivates your life. Revenge."

"Revenge? " said the Batman with surprise. "Is that what you think it is?"

"You do not agree?"

"I've always felt that my primary concern was for justice."

Sato shrugged. "Is that not the same thing?"

"I shouldn't think so," said the Batman.

"What is the difference?" Sato asked. "Justice done is punishment for wrong committed. Punishment is retribution. Retribution is revenge, is it not?"

"I've never thought of it quite that way."

"That is because revenge is not considered fashionable these days," Sato said. "Justice is merely a liberal term for the most conservative of concepts. I prefer to call a thing what it is."

"But if revenge and justice were really the same thing," the Batman said, "then I would seek to kill murderers, and I do not."

"That is because you are not a killer," said Sato simply. "Revenge, justice, call it what you will, may take many forms. It is not in your nature to kill, though you certainly possess the skill. It is one of the things about you that interests me the most. I have no compunctions about killing. If it is necessary, I will do it and my conscience will not trouble me. It is rarely necessary, yet I can easily conceive of situations where the necessity would arise. However, for you, it would be inconceivable."

The Batman nodded. "That's true. I could not take a human life."

"Why?"

"Because it would make me no different from the criminals I hunt."

Sato nodded. "And that is both your greatest weakness and your greatest strength. You are a man adept at violence, and yet you have a deep reverence for life. A man with one foot in the earthly world and one foot in the spiritual plane. Not entirely of one or of the other. You possess true Buddha-nature. It is something few men can achieve, and you are the only Westerner I have ever met who has achieved it. It is a thing I once aspired to myself, but I do not possess the proper qualities to walk that path. Many seek it, but few achieve the goal. You have never sought it, yet it has found you. Only, instead of bringing you transcendent joy, it torments you."

"You can see all that?" the Batman said softly.

"There are many ways of seeing," replied Sato. "It is why your outer face holds no importance for me. I can see the inner one quite clearly. I wish that I could bring you peace, my friend, but I fear that you shall never find it."

"Never?" said the Batman, his voice barely audible.

"You have taken the burdens of the world upon your shoulders," Sato said. "A truly stupid thing to do, but it is an honorable stupidity."

The Batman smiled. "So then Buddha-nature is a stupid thing. Is that what you're saying?"

"Of course it is a stupid thing. It is a foolish thing. It is impractical. It is not fashionable. It is neither logical nor governed by the ethics of the situation. But a foolish thing can sometimes be a good thing. I am not sure what I just said, but I suspect it is profound."

"You would have made either a great philosopher or a terrific stand-up comedian," said Batman with a grin.

Sato shrugged. "What's the difference?" He rose to his feet with a fluid motion. "Speaking of comedy," he said, "let us see if your sparring has improved any."

The Batman followed him out to the center of the dojo. They bowed once to the flags, once to each other, then each took a fighting stance. Actually, the Batman took a fighting stance. Sato simply stood there, arms hanging loosely at his sides. Suddenly, his right foot flashed up in a quadruple kick, four kicks in the same lightning, fluid motion—a front kick aimed at the midsection, a roundhouse to the temple, a reverse roundhouse to the opposite temple, and a side kick to the chin. It had the appearance of one devastatingly quick, sharp move, and the Batman succeeded in blocking the first three, but the last one caught him in the chin. He grunted and staggered. Sato hadn't pulled it.

"Pathetic," Sato said.

"Not bad for an old man," the Batman replied, rubbing his chin.

"No respect," said Sato, and at the same time he said it, he launched a furiously fast spinning crescent kick.

The Batman caught it, grabbed Sato's foot, and twisted sharply. It should have put him on his back, but rather than fight the leverage he exerted, Sato went with it and executed what looked like a sideways front flip, twisting his foot free and dropping down to sweep the Batman's feet out from under him. The Batman fell, rolled, and came quickly to his feet, in time to meet another furious attack, a series of spinning kicks that kept coming at him like a buzz saw as he blocked them all in rapid succession, backing away as he did so. Then suddenly he reversed his motion and moved into one of the kicks, trapping it with his body and dumping Sato on the floor. However, Sato pulled him along, flipping him over. The Batman somersaulted and landed on his feet. Sato produced a shuriken, as if from out of nowhere, and hurled it at him. The deadly throwing star arced toward him, and he jerked his head out of the way at the last instant. The shuriken's razor-sharp blades embedded themselves in the wall. In response, the Batman hurled a batarang.

Sato caught it one-handed and hurled it back. It was caught again.

They had progressed to weapons. Sato reached behind him and pulled out a pair of nunchuks. They whistled through the air as he manipulated them with astonishing speed. He pulled out a second pair. The Batman threw a smoke pellet on the floor. Sato waded straight into the cloud, but the Batman was no longer there. The nunchuks moved with a whistling blur as the cloud slowly dispersed, to reveal Sato standing alone in the center of the dojo.

For a moment he looked puzzled, then he suddenly looked up. His cape billowing out behind him, the Batman dropped on him from the ceiling. One pair of nunchuks went flying across the dojo to land with a clatter in a far corner of the loft. And then the Batman was flying through the air himself. He rolled as he landed, coming to his feet, and tossed four razorwings simultaneously. Sato batted each of the tiny projectiles out of the air with his whirling nunchuks.

This was no ordinary sparring session, and if any of Sato's students had been there to see it, they would have been breathless with amazement. There were two masters going all out, testing each other to the limits of their capabilities. Only two men supremely confident in each other's skills and reflexes could dare such unrestrained combat. The slightest error on the part of one of them could result in crippling injury, maybe even death, but each of them knew and trusted the abilities of his opponent. Only in this fashion could two supremely trained martial artists truly test their skills. There were few men alive who had achieved such a level. And it was this incredibly fast, brutal, and potentially deadly form of practice that defined the true nature of their relationship. In this lethal poetry of motion, they found joy and release. They reveled in each other's skill, putting on a show that any film producer would have paid a fortune for, but this was only for themselves. And had someone been there to capture it on film, no audience would ever have believed it. They would have been convinced that it was speeded-up trick photograhy and special effects. Finally, Sato cried out, *"Enough!"*

They both stood there, breathing heavily, almost completely spent. The Batman bowed. Sato bowed to him as well.

"Not . . . bad . . . for an . . . old man," said the Batman, grinning as he tried to catch his breath.

"If I were younger . . . you . . . would quickly learn . . . not to be . . . so insolent."

"How old . . . *are* you, anyway?" asked Batman.

"Old enough to collect . . . social security," Sato replied, "but still young enough to give you a good match."

"Amen to that," the Batman said. He shook his head, amazed, as always, at the old man's skill and endurance. "What a crime fighter you'd have made!"

"In another time . . . and in another place," said Sato, "but that was also in another life," he finished with a gesture of dismissal. "I am getting old and slow."

"Not so's I'd notice," the Batman replied. He bowed. "Thank you, Sensei."

"Thank *you*, my friend." The two men approached each other and embraced. "Come," said Sato when they broke apart, "we shall have another cup of tea. This has been thirsty work." He clapped the Batman on the shoulder, turned, and started heading back toward the table.

"Perhaps," said Sato, "You would care to join me for breakfast? I would be happy for the company." Receiving no reply, he turned and saw that he was suddenly alone in the dojo. He quickly glanced around, then expelled his breath sharply.

"He appears to be improving," he mumbled.

Commissioner Gordon's day started out badly and steadily got worse. Early that morning, a couple of officers in a patrol car had discovered two bodies slumped inside a late-model sedan with government plates. The dead men were FBI agents, part of Chambers's team, and both had been shot in the back of the head, through the rear windshield, by something that made mincemeat of their skulls. A short while later, a third body had been found, that of a well-dressed young woman, beneath the elevated highway. She, too, had been shot through the head, from the side, through the left temple. Ballistics hadn't come through with the report yet, but only one of the bullets had been found. It had gone completely through Jernigan's skull, had been deflected, and had lodged deep in the dashboard. The one that killed Palmer had continued on through the windshield, and the one that killed the third victim had also penetrated all the way through and had not been recovered.

Chambers again forgot to knock before he came barging into Gordon's office shortly after ten o'clock, but considering the circumstances, Gordon decided not to make a point of it. "We've got trouble," Chambers said.

"Coffee?" Gordon asked.

"Hell, yes," said Chambers, slumping down into a chair. Gordon made the call to Capiletti, then hung up the phone and turned to Chambers. The man looked terrible. He had large dark circles under his eyes, his clothes looked slept in, and his hair was uncombed. He had the look of a man on the edge of total exhaustion.

"Oh, I'm sorry, I forgot to knock," he said belatedly.

Gordon smiled. "Forget about it." Then the smile slipped from his face. "I'm very sorry about your men, Chambers. I've given instructions for the case to receive top priority. I've called ballistics personally and told them I want a report before noon today."

"The slugs were .45 Winchester Magnums, fired from a Grizzly Win Mag Mark 1 semiauto," Chambers said, gratefully accepting the cup of coffee from Sergeant Capiletti.

Gordon frowned. "What do you know that I don't?"

In response, Chambers tossed a manila folder onto Gordon's desk. "This just came in, courtesy of our friends at the CIA. The woman that got killed last night was one of theirs."

"She was a CIA agent?" Gordon said, picking up the folder and opening it.

"Lower echelon," said Chambers. "Marcia Davenport, intelligence analyst, based out of D.C. It looks as if she was doing a little freelance business on the side, selling information, and this time it backfired on her, so to speak. Needless to say, they're a bit embarrassed about the whole thing, which is why they're suddenly being so cooperative. The deal is we keep it quiet about what she was doing. I told them that would be no problem. Hope that's okay with you."

Gordon nodded. He glanced at the file. "What's Specter?" he asked.

"Not a what, a who," said Chambers. "You never saw that, by the way."

"Okay, who is he?"

"A professional assassin. According to the Company, he's just about the best there is. What little you've got there is all they know about him, and some of it they got from the KGB."

"The KGB?" said Gordon, raising his eyebrows. "You're joking."

"*Glasnost,*" Chambers said wryly. "Besides, they want him just as badly as we do. What's more, they're not particular about who takes him out. It seems some of the old guard in the Kremlin didn't like being asked to leave, so they tried to influence the new regime in the good, old-fashioned way. Some people got influenced permanently. Word is that Gorby had a narrow escape himself."

As Gordon scanned the file, he gave a low whistle.

"Makes impressive reading, doesn't it?" said Chambers. He shook his head. "And here I was, worried about the Batman."

"There's not much here, aside from information about suspected hits," said Gordon.

"What can I say, the bastard's good," said Chambers. "Most of his work has been abroad. Far as we know, he's never contracted in the States." He shrugged. "Far as we know. But the Russians know about him. He took out three of their best agents. Mention Specter to the

Mossad and they start foaming at the mouth. The Brits put out a bounty on him you could retire on, because of some wetwork he's done for the IRA. Son of a bitch has been tied to Bader-Meinhof, the Red Brigades, the PLO, and our good friends in Colombia, which also ties him to you-know-who."

"Desiderio Garcia," Gordon said.

'You got it. I just heard from the CIA about a half an hour ago. One of their field sections picked up the buzz that Specter's accepted a contract in the States. You remember that delicate political surveillance I spoke about the other day? Well, Miss Davenport was seen leaving a reception on the arm of certain UN diplomat last night. Five hours later, she turns up dead beneath the elevated highway. I have a feeling she was also photographed leaving that diplomat's apartment in the middle of the night, but somehow the film wound up getting exposed. Of course, you don't know anything about this. Mind if I smoke?"

"No, go right ahead," said Gordon.

Chambers took out a pack of cigarettes and lit one up. "I gave these up ten years ago," he said wryly. "Started again this morning."

"Needless to say, you can't question this diplomat because of immunity," said Gordon with a grimace. "You think maybe she was the bagman for a payoff?"

"I wouldn't be surprised. The kind of people she sold information to are the same kind of people who would employ someone like Specter. And Specter likes big, high-powered guns. Especially the Grizzly Win Mag."

"I must confess, I'm not familiar with the weapon," Gordon admitted. "I'm familiar with most revolvers and

9mm semiautos, but in my days on the streets, we all still carried .38's. And there was the occasional hot dog with a Government .45."

"That's basically what the Grizzly is," said Chambers. "It's patterned on the 1911 Government-model, only with all the competition bells and whistles and a wider, thicker grip to accommodate the magazines for some pretty potent rounds. It's chambered in your standard .45 ACP, in addition to .357, .357/45, 10mm, and .45 Winchester Magnum. All calibers interchangeable. It's not exactly your standard hit man's cheap, throwaway item. A lot of serious shooters lay out some pretty heavy bucks to gunsmiths to slick up their pistols for competition. The Grizzly comes that way right from the factory. It can accept a compensator and a silencer, and it's extremely well made. Right here in the good ole U.S. of A."

"And it's Specter's trademark gun?"

"Yeah," said Chambers, exhaling a long stream of smoke, "He just loves that big .45 Magnum round. It'll put down a bear, which is where the pistol gets its name, I guess. Specter doesn't like to leave any room for error."

Gordon exhaled heavily. "Just what we need," he said. "A terrorist on the loose in Gotham City."

"Specter's not your average terrorist," said Chambers. "Terrorists are fanatics for a cause. Specter doesn't have a cause. He's a pro. And the measure of his status in the game is that he's made over sixty big-time hits and nobody even has the faintest idea what he looks like."

"Somebody must know," said Gordon. "How else can he do business?"

"He deals through intermediaries," Chambers replied. "You want somebody taken out, you put the word out through the right channels. And I'm not talking about your mob-type grapevine. I'm talking arms merchants and mercenaries and international drug cartels. Specter gets in touch with you and tells *you* to appoint a middleman—or woman—who'll be the contact for the deal. And if you know anything about the way he operates, you'll pick someone expendable."

"Sounds like a charming guy," said Gordon dryly. "But how's he going to find a secret witness who's in federal protective custody?"

"That's the bad news," Chambers said.

"You mean everything you've told me up to now has been the *good* news?" Gordon said.

Chambers grimaced. "The Company masterminded the Garcia snatch," he said. "We just came in on the tail end of the deal, to handle the logistics through the trial and relocate the witness in the program. Of course, that means the Company knows all the detail of the operation."

"The people breathing down your neck," said Gordon, remembering the other day's discussion.

"Exactly," Chambers said. "And Davenport worked for the Company as an analyst. Which means she had top clearance, with access to computer files and all interdepartmental communication."

"Hell," said Gordon.

"Hell is right," said Chambers. "Our security's completely blown. And where there was one leak—"

"There could be more," said Gordon. He grimaced. "What can I do to help?"

"I was hoping you would ask me that," said Chambers. "I'd like you to take charge of the witness."

"You mean take over the security?" asked Gordon.

"No, I mean take the witness," Chambers said. "Your department's cleaned up its act better than just about any other large city. You've got one hell of a good rep, and frankly, Commissioner, I trust you. Right about now, I don't know too many other people I can trust."

"I can see your point," said Gordon. "But if I'm going to do this, Chambers, I'm going to have to do it *my* way."

"Hey, you got it."

"Hear me out first," Gordon said. "Your security's already been compromised, and I'm not going to put my officers at risk. You hand over the witness according to my terms, and I'll put my very best people on the job. But neither the Bureau nor the CIA is going to know where that witness will be kept. And that includes everyone in my department who's not directly on the job. It also includes you."

"*Me?* Hey, now come on..."

"I mean it," Gordon said. "It's like you told me the other day. What you don't know can't hurt you. You can't be ordered to reveal where the witness is if you don't know. That's the deal. Take it or leave it."

Chambers took a deep breath and let it out slowly. "All right, I'll take it. I don't like it, but I'll take it. There's too much at stake not to. But if anything happens to my witness, I don't need to tell you that both your ass and mine will fry."

"I understand that," Gordon said. "Give me a few hours to work out the details and I'll get back to you."

"Right," said Chambers, stubbing out his cigarette and getting up. "Don't take too long, okay? If my superiors find out about this, they might try to stop it."

"Two hours," Gordon said.

Chambers nodded. "All right." He sighed heavily. "I'm probably going to catch hell for this, but I don't want to take any chances. I just hope I'm not making a mistake."

He left and closed the door. "So do I," said Gordon softly. He picked up the phone. "Capiletti? Find Lieutenant Carman. Tell him to drop whatever's he doing and get to my office *now*. Ditto Detective Heintzelman, Detective Cruz, Sergeant Mallory, and Sergeant Rondell. I want them all here within twenty minutes, ready for duty."

He put down the phone and his gaze fell on the corner of his desk, where Agent Chambers had left behind his cigarettes. He reached out and picked them up, holding the pack in his hand thoughtfully. Then he put them in his pocket.

CHAPTER
FOUR

"GOOD evening, I'm Roger Greeley and here is tonight's news. Early this morning, the bodies of two FBI agents were discovered in their car near the West Side elevated highway, by the waterfront. The slain men have been identified as agents Jeffrey Davis Palmer and Ronald M. Jernigan. They had been shot, execution-style, while apparently pursuing an investigation closely related to the Garcia case. For further details, we go to Jerri Downing, at police headquarters. Jerri?"

The camera cut to an attractive blond woman with a feathered hairdo and the look of a fashion model.

"Roger, the details on the murder of the two federal agents last night are, at this point, extremely sketchy, and the authorities are being very closemouthed about the case. We have learned that there was a third body found near the scene"—she quickly consulted her notes—"that of a woman named Marcia Davenport, tentatively identified as a government employee. Precisely what her connection was with the Garcia case, assuming there *was* a connection, cannot be established at this point. Gotham City FBI Bureau Chief Reese Chambers was not available for comment, but reporters caught up with Commissioner James Gordon as he was leaving police headquarters tonight."

They went to a tape of Gordon walking down the stairs outside the building and suddenly being swarmed by reporters with their microphones held out like weapons.

"Commissioner Gordon! Commissioner!" They all tried to shout their questions at once. "Commissioner, what can you tell us about the murder of those two FBI agents last night?"

"At this point, all I can tell you is that the department is cooperating fully with the FBI in the investigation," Gordon said. "We intend to give the Bureau all possible assistance."

"Commissioner, do you have any idea why those men were killed? Did it have anything to do with the Garcia case?"

"I wouldn't wish to speculate on that," Gordon replied. "Those men were FBI agents, not Gotham City police officers, and as such, I am not aware of whether or not they were engaged in any investigation at the time of their deaths."

"Would the FBI have told you if they were?"

"I am not in a position to speculate as to what the FBI may or may not have done in the context of any investigation they might have been pursuing," said Gordon.

"Commissioner Gordon, is there any connection between the murders of those agents and that of Ms. Davenport, since they occurred in the same vicinity?"

"There are certain similarities," said Gordon, "but at this point in time, we do not yet have access to the ballistics reports, and as a result, we cannot say conclusively that the murders were connected. However, we are certainly not ruling out that possibility."

"Commissioner, were the murdered agents connected with Ms. Davenport? She's been identified as a government employee, which is not very specific. Could you tell us anything more about that? Exactly in what capacity did she work for government?"

"That's something I can't answer at this point," said Gordon. "I am not directly involved in the investigation, but I fully intend to keep abreast of all developments."

"Commissioner, from what we've been told about the murders, they appear to have all the earmarks of a professional assassination. Wouldn't that indicate a strong possibility of a connection with the Garcia case?"

"Well, anything is possible," said Gordon, "but as I've already said, I don't wish to engage in speculation. I think that would be counterproductive."

"Sir, we've heard rumors that a contract has been put out on the government witness against General Garcia. In light of these execution-style murders, and the fact that the victims were government personnel, is it possible that the security of that witness has been compromised?"

Gordon frowned. "I'm afraid I couldn't answer that question. I am not familiar with the details of any security arrangements that the FBI may or may not have regarding any possible witnesses in the Garcia case.

That's something that would concern the FBI, and I'm not in a position to speak for them.''

"Commissioner, do you have any knowledge if the murdered woman, Ms. Davenport, was working for the FBI or for the CIA?"

"I couldn't comment on that."

"But you're not saying that she *wasn't*?"

"What I said was that I could make no comment one way or the other."

"Commissioner, to your knowledge is the government witness against General Garcia still safe and in the custody of the FBI somewhere in Gotham City?"

"As I've already said several times, I'm not in a position to speak for the FBI. I am not familiar with the particulars of any arrangements or investigations they may or may not be involved in regarding the Garcia case. The case of General Garcia falls under federal jurisdiction, and anything that pertains to that case is the provincc of thc federal authorities, not the Gotham City Police Department."

"Commissioner, is there any truth to the rumor that the Gotham City Police Department, specifically your office, has been asked to assume custody of the witness against General Garcia, due to a possible breach in security?"

The camera zoomed in for a close shot of Gordon as his lips tightened into an angry grimace.

"I repeat, I am not in a position to either confirm or deny any rumors related to the Garcia case," he replied. "The Bureau has asked us not to release any information or make any comment concerning the Garcia case or anything related to it, and the department's policy has always been to cooperate with federal agencies."

"But is it true, Commissioner?" a reporter persisted.

"Is there something wrong with your hearing?" Gordon asked testily.

"So you're not denying that the FBI has requested your assistance in protecting the witness?" someone else called out.

"I suggest you ask the FBI," said Gordon, trying to push his way through the crowd of reporters. "Now, if you'll excuse me...."

"One moment, Commissioner! I have something here I think you ought to hear."

The shot widened out to show Enrique Vasquez, a grandstanding young reporter for a rival network, standing at the foot of the stairs and confronting Gordon.

"Yes, Mr. Vasquez," Gordon said in a tone of obvious displeasure. "What is it?"

"A short while ago, Commissioner, I received a call at the newsroom, the text of which I think you ought to hear. The caller said, and I quote, "This is Specter. Your government authorities can tell you who I am, and can vouch for my professional reputation. I have already dispatched several of your government agents who got in my way. I am hereby serving notice on the federal authorities, and on the people of Gotham City, that if General Desiderio Garcia is not released within twenty-four hours and provided with an aircraft that will fly him to Cuba, I will commence indiscriminate terrorist actions against the people of Gotham City. One life for many. The choice is yours." And then the caller hung up. Would you care to comment on that, Commissioner?"

Uncharacteristically, every single reporter fell silent, awaiting Gordon's response. The corner of Gordon's mouth twitched. He took out a pack of cigarettes and put one in his mouth.

Bruce Wayne suddenly sat forward in his chair. His eyes were intent upon the screen.

"The only comment I have to make, Mr. Vasquez," Gordon said tensely, lighting his cigarette, "is that what you have just done demonstrates a lack of journalistic integrity and an irresponsibility that reaches a new low, even for you." His hand shook slightly as he took the cigarette out of his mouth and blew out the smoke in a sharp, angry burst, apparently without having bothered to inhale it. "Some crank *allegedly* makes a phone call to your newsroom, and without bothering to inform the police, or substantiate your highly dubious so-called source, you go on the air with this irresponsible nonsense and risk frightening the people of this city and creating a panic. I am frankly astonished at your callousness and gall."

"But what if it *isn't* nonsense, Commissioner?" Vasquez persisted, apparently unruffled by the dressing-down. "If that call from this individual calling himself 'Specter' turns out to be tragically on the level, what are you going to tell the people of this city?"

"I don't deal in uninformed speculation, Mr. Vasquez," Gordon replied. "I deal in facts."

"The *fact*, Commissioner," Vasquez continued, seeking to block his way, "is that when I contacted the headquarters of the FBI shortly after receiving that call, and I asked them who this 'Specter' was, their response was, 'No comment.' Not that they never *heard* of anyone called Specter, but 'No comment.' What is your response to that?''

"For the last time, I can't answer for the FBI, Mr. Vasquez," Gordon replied. "Nor am I responsible for your dramatic interpretations of anything that they might have said to you. And now, if you'll excuse me, I have nothing more to say."

He tossed aside the cigarette and shoved his way past the reporters.

Bruce Wayne turned off the television and got up out of the chair. Jim Gordon did not smoke cigarettes. He smoked a pipe.

The cigarettes had been a signal, one of a number of signals they had worked out between them. Another was any police radio dispatch that mentioned "Car 13." There was no "Car 13" in the Gotham City Police Department, for the same reason that many hotels did not have a thirteenth floor. No explanation was ever given to the rank-and-file police for why the mythical "Car 13" came up from time to time, and many of them assumed it was some sort of private signal to somebody, but none of them every suspected who that somebody actually was.

While in the Batmobile he always monitored the police band, and in the Batcave he had another monitor, which taped the dispatches and was hooked up to a computer that instantly flagged any dispatch that mentioned "Car 13" and logged the time and date.

He came into the kitchen, where Alfred was preparing

dinner. "Something's come up, Alfred," he said. "I have to go below."

"Shall I wait with dinner, Master Bruce?" asked Alfred.

"I don't know, I'll call you from below," he replied.

"Very well, sir." Alfred sighed as Bruce approached the large stainless-steel, wood-paneled refrigerator and opened the door. "Have you ever considered, sir, installing a dumbwaiter so that I might send you down a sandwich now and then so you don't waste away?"

"That's not a bad idea, Alfred," Bruce said, reaching inside the refrigerator and working the temperature-control dial as if it were a combination lock, which was exactly what it was. "Why don't you get to work on that?"

Alfred raised his eyes toward the ceiling and sighed. "Somehow, I knew you'd say that. Yet *another* home-improvement project. I wonder if we have enough explosive left over from the last one."

"Just think of all the walking up and down the stairs it'll save you," Bruce said as he finished turning the dial and closed the refrigerator door.

There was a muffled clicking sound, followed by the subdued whine of servo motors as the entire refrigerator began to retract into the wall, sliding back on steel rails set flush with the floor. It slid straight back about five feet and stopped. He stepped into the opening. Directly to his right, behind the built-in cabinets and the wall to the right of the refrigerator, was what appeared to be a small closet with no door. He stepped into it and punched the lower of two black buttons in a small control panel. The elevator started to descend through the rough stone shaft. He stepped out into a narrow, carpeted hallway with several doors leading off it to either side.

It might have been the hallway of an office building, except that it was too narrow and too short. Two people would have had to go down it single file. The walls of the hallway, which ended in a door at the far end, were paneled in dark wood, and the indirect lighting was subdued. Several of the doors gave access to finished, comfortable rooms, without any windows.

One was a small library, isolated from the dampness of the Batcave, that held the sort of books Bruce Wayne would not have in his library upstairs. Another was an arsenal, containing a wide variety of small arms mounted on the walls; military ordnance such as fully automatic assault rifles, carbines, and machine pistols, in addition to revolvers and semiautomatics and even derringers. The Batman was an expert with each of these weapons, though he never used any of them except for purposes of research. The door at the far end of the corridor led to the Batcave's main computer and central control room.

This room was thermostatically controlled and its walls were glass, affording a panoramic view of the Batcave. It was set well above the cavern floor, with a door leading to an exit on the right side. It opened onto a long flight of steps cut into the stone, curving around the front of the large rock formation on which the control room had been constructed. Visible from the control room was the entire main chamber of the cavern where the Batman made his home.

Few had ever seen the Batcave, but of those who did, no one ever forgot it. The construction of the hidden sanctuary was impressive, all the more so when one considered that most of the work had been performed by only two men, the Batman himself and Alfred Pennyworth. There were some parts of the project that had been too big and complicated for just two men to handle, such as the massive blast doors that gave access to the long tunnel that allowed the Batmobiles to leave and enter unobserved, the hidden doors for the hangar concealed in the hillside near Wayne Manor, the heavy, hydraulic lifts, and the large, automated turntables for the Batmobiles, the Batcoper, and the Batplane. It had been necessary to employ a small labor force for such elements of the construction, but the security precautions that had been taken to guard the secrets of the Batcave had been as elaborate as those practiced by the pharaohs in the construction of their tombs.

The workers had all been recruited in the Far East, from construction companies owned through several corporate blinds by WayneTech Enterprises. The arrangements were so byzantine that it would have been nearly impossible to unravel them, even had anyone known where to begin. Each of the workers had been cleared through exhaustive security checks, and none of them had spoken English. They had been picked up in the Orient and flown aboard a private transport that departed from a hidden airfield. None of them had even the vaguest clue as to their destination, but they were paid a fortune for their services and for their silence. Even if they had chosen to disregard their promise about silence, they wouldn't have had very much to tell.

The contract they had agreed to stipulated that they would be sedated for their journey, so they would have no way of knowing how long it had taken. The plane on which they had arrived landed at a secluded private airstrip, and was immediately taken inside a hangar, where the sedated work force was carefully transferred into two fully enclosed trucks. Throughout their journey, Alfred had carefully monitored their condition. They were then taken by truck to the Batcave, with Alfred driving one truck and Bruce driving the other. They came to inside the cavern, with absolutely no idea of where they were. They did not know what country it was, in what part of the world or even whether it was day or night.

None of them had ever seen the Batman. Throughout the project, their overseers were Alfred Pennyworth, his appearance disguised with makeup, and Bruce Wayne, in his disguise as "Matches" Malone, a gangster whose identity he had adopted as a sometime alias after the real Malone was killed. All the necessary equipment and supplies had been purchased through companies owned by WayneTech, and throughout the construction project, the work force had been quartered in the Batcave, all their needs and comforts seen to. The only time they ever went outside was when they installed the hangar doors and the blast doors. In both those cases, the work had been performed at night, with only the work areas illuminated, so that they could tell almost nothing about their surroundings. Once the work was completed, they were taken back the same way they had come, many of them convinced that they had participated in some sort of secret military project. However, the money they were paid had been more than enough to assuage their curiosity.

With the main portion of the project taken care of, Bruce Wayne and Alfred Pennyworth had then completed the finishing touches by themselves. They had installed state-of-the-art computer equipment and brought it on line, set up the repair shop and the lab with sophisticated equipment purchased through WayneTech and its subsidiaries, and put in a complete gym, with weights and exercise machines and gymnastic apparatus that would allow the Batman to keep in fighting trim. It had taken a long time, and over the years, the equipment and the setup of the Batcave had evolved to meet the needs of the world's most high-tech vigilante.

Finally, only one thing remained to be done. Knowledge of the cavern system itself had to be kept secret. From childhood, Bruce had remembered his father telling him that the existence of the caverns underneath Wayne Manor was not generally known. Thomas Wayne, for all his success as a brilliant surgeon, had not been a self-made man. The Waynes were one of the oldest families in the city's social register, and they could trace their ancestry back all the way to the Pilgrims of the Mayflower. The Waynes had built up their fortune over many years, and the estate had been in the family for generations. And, for generations, the Waynes had carefully guarded their privacy.

Several of the early members of the family had apparently discovered the caverns and explored them, but young Andrew Wayne IV, descended from the famous Revolutionary War general, "Mad Anthony" Wayne, had been killed in a fall when he had stumbled into a deep crevice in the lower reaches of the cavern system. The story had survived in the family's writings. Ever since, Thomas Wayne had told his son, the family had kept the existence of the caverns secret, for fear that knowledge of them would attract not only geologists, but amateur spelunkers and local kids who could easily meet the fate of Andrew Wayne.

"The caverns are very dangerous, Bruce," his father had told him, "and we have a responsibility to make sure that no one knows about them, so that no one else can get hurt or killed down there."

But what if records of the caves' existence could be found somewhere? What if, at some time in the past, a geologic survey had been made? Bruce Wayne had to make certain that no information existed that could lead to the discovery of the Batcave. Using both his computer system and researching through public government, and university libraries, he had carefully and painstakingly made certain that no record of the caverns existed anywhere.

Now, as he entered the main control room of his sanctuary, he was secure in the inviolability of his domain. His entire manner changed as he came into the Batcave. The casual, insouciant slouch of Bruce Wayne disappeared, replaced by the erect, perfect posture of the Batman, who moved with supple grace and the coil-spring tension of the perfect athlete. It was not a conscious change, but something that had become second nature with him. Bruce Wayne and the Batman were two completely differently personalities, one an elaborate, well-developed facade, the other the driven man within, whom few people would ever really know.

He checked the equipment that monitored the police band and, sure enough, a call had gone out for "Car 13." That, combined with the cigarette signal Gordon had used, knowing the Batman always watched the news, could only mean one thing. The signal Gordon had used on camera had been given when Enrique Vasquez revealed the communication from Specter, who had taken credit for the murders of the FBI agents, and possibly had murdered Marcia Davenport, the "government employee" who was probably an agent of either the FBI or the CIA, just as the reporters had assumed. The call for "Car 13" had gone out shortly thereafter. Gordon must have ordered it from his car. To the Batman, that meant Gordon had probably already known about this Specter when Vasquez brought it up. So it was on the level.

The Batman sat down behind the computer console. From this console, he could access any data bank, almost anywhere in the world. And he had a considerable data bank of his own. WayneTech manufactured electronic hardware, and produced software to run it, for some of the largest multinational corporations in the world. With computer hackers growing more and more sophisticated and computer crime a worldwide concern, WayneTech produced state-of-the-art safeguard programs that were virtually undefeatable. Hidden deep within the systems were secret codes that gave the Batman access. And any data banks that were not protected by a WayneTech safeguard system were easy for the Batman to break into. Had he wanted to, he could have been the biggest computer criminal in the entire world, but his knowledge was tempered by a great sense of responsibility, and the strictest of moral codes.

He first checked his own data banks for any references to "Specter" and came up with nothing. This did not surprise him. He could not recall ever having heard of anyone who called himself Specter, and so, he would not have entered any such data into his system. He then entered a sequence of commands that would instruct his program to run a search through the databases of the FBI, CIA, NSA, Britain's MI-6, Israel's Mossad, and Interpol, the databases most likely to contain information about international terrorists and assassins. His one regret was that he had no access to the records of the KGB—not because the Russians were too clever, but because their information-storage systems were so hopelessly outdated. The most sophisticated computer program in the world could not open a file drawer.

The commands entered and the program running, now there was nothing to do but sit back and wait. It would take some time. In the near future, he hoped to be able to upgrade his equipment with an optical computer system based not on electrons, but on photons. Information could then be retrieved at the speed of light. WayneTech was currently working with a prototype of such a system, but until the technology became widespread, it would take time, even for the Batman, to search through highly classified storage systems. It would be a few hours, at least, before he could go and see Jim Gordon.

If Specter was really on the level, and it certainly appeared as if he was, then whoever he was, he was either well-informed about events and personalities in Gotham City or he had access to someone who could give him the information he required. If he had wanted to make his announcement through the media he could not have picked a better messenger than Enrique Vasquez. A cocky, bantam rooster of a man, Vasquez had first been a crime reporter. He made much of his growing up "on the streets" and his knowledge of the gang scene. He brought a hip, streetwise, flamboyant flair to his stories, and his courage—some called it foolhardiness—in covering his stories, coupled with his dark good looks, soon made him a well-known personality. He became a "crusading reporter," but his chief crusade seemed to be a quest for fame, and he took every opportunity to get a scoop that would advance his own career, often regardless of the consequences. A responsible journalist, on receiving such a call, would have first contacted the police and tried to verify whether it was a real threat or simply some crank trying to get publicity. Vasquez went right on the air with it in a manner guaranteed to get him maximum exposure. Whoever Specter was, he had played the reporter like a fish.

Of all crimes, terrorism was the most difficult to defend against. Was Specter an individual or was he part of some organization? The Batman had never heard of an organization known as Specter. There was a similar-sounding one in the writings of Ian Fleming, but that was fiction. This Specter sounded all too real. And the message Vasquez had read made Specter sound as if he was an individual. However, the Batman wasn't about to depend for his information on someone like Enrique Vasquez.

While he waited for the data to come in, he sat down behind another console and started typing in commands. It couldn't hurt to find out exactly which branch of government service the late Marcia Davenport had been employed in. Given the many tentacles of government bureaucracy, it could have been a time-consuming task, but the Batman played a hunch. The FBI, except in cases of undercover work, did not generally make a point of concealing the identity of their agents. That sounded more like the CIA. It was a relatively simple matter to access the agency's personnel records. Bingo. Davenport, Marcia Anne. Social security number, photo, personnel data. Intelligence analyst. Level 6 clearance.

Interesting. Not exactly the sort of person the CIA would use for intelligence work in the field. But on the other hand, a person with access to the kind of information she worked with every day could conceivably decide to make some money on the side, selling that information. And if Marcia Davenport had been suspected of selling secrets, it could explain why the FBI would have been interested in her. But what was she doing in Gotham City? She was based in Washington. Why go to Gotham City when she could have worked out clandestine meetings and dead drops with foreign-embassy personnel right in the nation's capital? Unless, of course, her presence in Gotham City had nothing to do with selling classified information.

The other data he'd requested started to come in. Within moments, the Batman had essentially the same information contained in the report Chambers had given to Jim Gordon. And then some. The activities of Specter were well known to Britain's MI-6. Also to the Mossad, and Interpol, and French Intelligence, and, indirectly, to the CIA. Whoever he was, Specter seemed to have confined his activities primarily to the European continent, the British Isles, and the Middle East. And whoever he was, he was definitely a pro. A pro who was so good at his job that almost nothing was known about him. He had chosen his name well. He was like a ghost. Wherever he appeared, death and destruction followed, and then he simply vanished without a trace.

It looked as if this was his first visit to America. And judging by the results of his sojourns elsewhere, he would soon be announcing his arrival with a vengeance.

It was a small walk-up apartment on the fourth floor, what was known as a "railroad flat," with all the rooms lined up in a row. The entrance from the hall led into the kitchen. Through an alcove was the living room, which had a small bathroom off to one side. And the living room led into the bedroom which had two windows leading out onto the fire escape. There was easy access to the roof, either up the fire escape or up one flight of stairs inside the building, and it was a simple matter to cross over to the roofs of the adjoining buildings. It was not the most secure setup in the world, but it would do.

He had answered the ad in the *Gotham Voice* and subletted the small apartment in the Village from a couple of musicians who had shared it. Their band would be on tour for the next six months, opening for a larger act, and being pressed for time, they had been all too pleased to find a tenant, especially one who had paid the damage deposit and the full six months' rent up front, in cash.

He had told them he was an assistant to an independent London film producer who had a property in development that would require some shooting in the States. He was in town to set things up, scout locations, and straighten out the film permits and so forth. He had a great deal to do, and didn't really wish to be bothered with every would-be actor in the city pestering him for a part in the film. So he had hinted that if they refrained from telling anyone about him there might be work for them when they came back from their tour, scoring some of the music for the film.

They had reassured him that they would be the souls of discretion, and if there was anything that they could do to make things easier for him before they left, such as setting him up with some female company, for instance, or perhaps a connection for some "dynamite blow," all he needed was to say the word. He had declined politely, saying perhaps when they returned, but for now, he had a great deal of work to do and would have little free time to himself. Perhaps when they returned from their tour, and he had everything taken care of, there would be time to party.

The first thing he had done was install new locks. Musicians were an easygoing bunch, and there was no telling to whom they might have given keys. He then checked to make sure the rock and rollers had disconnected the phone before they left. He did not intend to reestablish service. Any calls he would make would be made from public phones, and never from the same location twice. After that, he began to gather his supplies, most of which he bought himself at various retail outlets in the city, carefully spreading the purchases out in such a way as to make them seem perfectly innocuous, while others he acquired through burglarizing warehouses belonging to construction companies, which he had located through the phone book. He did everything methodically, with careful planning and flawless execution. When he had acquired everything he needed, he made the telephone call to that reporter on the TV news. By then, of course, he had already picked out his first target and made all the preparations.

He had no doubt that they would eventually give in to his demands and release Garcia. These were Americans, after all, not the Israelis or the British, who were considerably more hard-nosed about such things. The Americans were soft. They were loud and boorish and liked to flex their muscles. They were good at hiring others to do their fighting for them or invading tiny island nations, but anytime their own comfort and security was threatened, they turned spineless. They would seek to negotiate and they would stall for time, hoping that somehow the crisis would resolve itself, and in the end, if they could not intimidate their way to the desired result, they would cave in. His greatest weapon on this contract would be the American people themselves, especially their media. But he would first have to make his presence felt.

His first act would demonstrate his serious intent. And then would come the second, and the third, and the fourth, timed and executed in a way that would ensure maximum impact, and soon the populace would be clamoring for General Garcia to be freed. In the meantime, their authorities would be stomping around like stormtroopers in jackboots, making a great deal of noise to no effect, and in the process they would make mistakes. Mistakes that he could take advantage of. In fact, he hadn't even started yet and they had already made one very large mistake.

He had watched the news, to make certain his message was delivered. That reporter the ambassador had recommended would be useful. His vanity would make him the perfect pawn.

He had intended to put pressure on the FBI by allowing them to find Marcia's body. It had alerted them to the fact that their security was compromised, as he had known it would. They would now panic and immediately start changing their arrangements. With any luck, in their haste they would do something to give themselves away, because unfortunately Marcia had not been able to discover where the government witness was being kept.

She had verified that there was, indeed, a witness, whom the FBI rather quaintly referred to by the code name "Songbird," and she had learned the nature of the testimony this witness would give in exchange for immunity and relocation in the federal witness protection program. But somewhere along the line, she'd stumbled and tipped off her superiors before she could get all the details of where the witness was being hidden. She had been frightened, and he knew she was about to run. She had stopped being useful and had become a liability. It had been necessary to eliminate her, which was what he had intended all along, but it was inconvenient that she had not been able to get him all the information he required.

Instead, he'd had it practically handed to him on a platter, thanks to the American media. Police Commissioner Gordon might very well be an able administrator, but he was not a very good liar. When the reporters had asked him if the police were going to take custody of the witness from the FBI, his facial expression and his body language had given him away. Perhaps someone in the FBI or the police department had been careless and the information had leaked out, or perhaps the press had simply stumbled on that possibility all on their own, but either way, Gordon's reaction to that question had been very revealing. He had attempted to dissemble, but he wasn't very good at it.

And it made perfect sense. The American CIA had always been obsessed with secrecy, especially given the open nature of their society, and it was well known that they did not make a habit of telling the FBI what they were doing. The two agencies had always been competitive, and there was little love lost between them. With the knowledge that CIA duplicity had compromised their operation, it would only be logical for the FBI to take steps to ensure the security of the witness they were protecting. And what better way to do that than to allow the Gotham City police to take custody of the witness? It was their city, after all, and with their history of organized crime and their system of plea bargaining with informers, they would doubtless have suitable safe houses already established. Safe houses that the CIA and, for that matter, the FBI would know nothing about. It was an effective way of circumventing any leaks within their own organization, and, if anything should happen to the witness, the blame would fall not on them, but on the Gotham City police. Yes, it made perfect sense.

It also played right into his hands. He would pressure the American government into releasing Garcia and dispose of the witness against him at the same time. All in all, it would be a neat and profitable little enterprise, one that would enhance his standing immeasurably.

He would now focus his attention on Police Commissioner James Gordon.

CHAPTER
FIVE

IT was almost midnight when Jim Gordon pulled into the overlook near the entrance to the Arkham Asylum. It had been a short drive across the bridge and up the parkway that ran along the river. Once he was over the bridge, the urban sprawl of Gotham City had given way to wooded countryside. Commuters from the fashionable suburbs of Gotham City choked this route during the morning and the evening rush hours, but most other times it was lightly traveled, and at this hour traffic was almost nonexistent. The interchange to the upstate parkway had been passed a few miles back, and most of the late night traffic had been left behind. He drove along the wooded bluffs above the river and pulled into a certain scenic overlook, from which one could see the Gotham Bridge in the distance and, beyond it, the lights of the city across the river.

Occasionally, a couple of young lovers might be

discovered parked here, but it was a simple matter to flash his shield and tell them to move on. On this occasion, the graveled overlook was deserted. About a mile farther up the parkway, a road branched off to the left that led to the Arkham Asylum. This asylum for the criminally insane occupied the grounds of a sprawling old estate, and its presence in the area had forestalled development in the vicinity. No one wanted to live anywhere near the place. It was about as isolated an area as one could find.

He parked his car, got out, and lit his pipe. He looked out across the river toward the city in the distance. Somewhere out there, he thought, an international terrorist was loose, a remorseless professional assassin who had left a trail of death all over Europe. If he had anything to say about it, that trail would end here in Gotham City. But in order to make that come about, he needed help.

In a short while, he heard the sound of an approaching car. Only, it was not just any car. The muted, high-pitched whine of its engine did not sound like anything that left the assembly lines in Hamamatsu or Detroit. It could only be the Batmobile.

He turned and saw it pulling into the overlook. This latest incarnation of the Batmobile was black and sleek, like all the others that had preceded it, but it was smaller, with a body that was aerodynamically rounded. Its lines were a cross between a Ferrari F40 and a Lamborghini Diablo, the two most exotic production automobiles in the world, only this car could blow the doors off both of them. And it was equipped with "options" that even the most well-heeled Ferraristi could only dream of. The car looked like a rocket even standing still, but when its driver floored the accelerator, the G force pressed you back in the ergonomically contoured seat as if you were an astronaut lifting off from Cape Canaveral.

The door opened and the Caped Crusader stepped out, blending into the darkness like a shadow. Gordon couldn't see him clearly until he was almost within reach of him.

"You wanted to see me, Jim?" said the deep, familiar voice.

As always, Gordon was struck by the presence of the man. The Batman was six feet, two inches tall, with a weight of about two hundred and forty pounds, not an ounce of which was fat. He had the physique of a champion bodybuilder. But it was more than just his size; it was the way he held himself, the way he moved, the way he spoke. Everything about him gave the impression of a commanding self-confidence, which was all the more emphasized by his dark, dramatic attire. His deep voice had resonance and timbre. He moved with an utter economy of motion, without any of the fidgeting or slouching mannerisms that most people had. The impression he gave was that of a man completely in control. It was impossible to be in his presence and not feel a sort of awe.

"I was afraid you wouldn't come," said Gordon.

"Have I ever failed you?"

"No," Gordon replied, "you haven't. But each time, I think, what if *this* time, he won't be there?"

"I'll always be there for you, Jim. You know that. It's about Specter, isn't it?"

"You know about him?"

"Until a short while ago, I didn't," replied the Batman, "but I've since taken a cram course. And what I've learned has me very worried."

"How much do you know?" asked Gordon.

"At least as much as you, and possibly more," the Batman said. "Unfortunately, none of it is very helpful. Whoever Specter is, he's covered his tracks well. He appears to be the consummate professional. Cold, calculating, and utterly ruthless."

"That was my impression, too, when I saw the CIA's file on him," Gordon said. "But we've got to stop him somehow. I was hoping I could count on your help."

"You have it," said the Batman. "But I'm afraid there's little we can do to stop him at the moment." He sighed heavily and looked away toward the distant city. "Innocent people are going to die, Jim."

"I've organized a task force," Gordon said, "which will be advised by Agent Chambers. He's the one in charge of the security around Garcia."

"Yes, I know," the Batman said. "I suggest you see if you can get some cooperation from the intelligence agencies of some of the countries Specter had been active in. They may have people who might be better able to advise you. I have nothing against Chambers, I don't know the man, but he hasn't had any experience with Specter. Perhaps someone from M1-6, or the Mossad . . ."

"I've already put that in motion," Gordon said, "but what with bureaucratic red tape and all, it'll take time. And time is something we haven't got. He's given the government a twenty-four-hour deadline to release Garcia and then . . . well, the implication is clear."

The Batman nodded. "He'll seek to make a dramatic

demonstration, something that will terrify the people of Gotham City and forcibly bring home to them how vulnerable they are. It will most likely be a bomb.''

''Yes, but where?'' asked Gordon helplessly.

''Anywhere where it can do the maximum amount of damage,'' said the Batman, ''and take a significant number of lives. Unfortunately, in Gotham City that could be almost anywhere. That's the hell of terrorism. It's almost impossible to defend against.''

''I know,'' said Gordon with a sinking feeling. ''The thought that in less then twenty-four hours...'' His voice trailed off. ''He probably already has his first bomb planted. And it could be anywhere. Anywhere at all.''

''That's not all that worries me,'' the Batman said. ''You're in danger yourself, Jim.''

''Me?''

''If you take custody of the government witness,'' said the Batman, ''Specter could come after you.''

''Let him try,'' said Gordon with a hard edge to his voice.

''It's not just you, Jim,'' said the Batman. ''You've got family. Specter could try to get at you through them.''

Gordon paled. ''My God. I hadn't thought of that.''

''I've got an idea,'' said the Batman. ''One that will eliminate that danger and might flush out this Specter. Let *me* take the witness.''

''*You?*'' said Gordon with astonishment.

''That's right. Can you think of a safer place to hide a federal witness than the Batcave?''

''Impossible,'' said Gordon, shaking his head. ''Chambers would never agree to it. He's already taking a big chance by letting us take over. He's probably going to catch hell from his superiors at the Bureau, and he knows it. But his back's against the wall. He can't take a chance on losing that witness. He was even worried about you! And if I took it upon myself and let you have the witness, it would mean my job. My career would be finished if anyone even suspected I was working with you, much less—"

"You don't have to let me *have* the witness, Jim," the Batman interrupted him. "Nobody says it has to be done with your official cooperation."

"I don't understand."

"Correct me if I'm wrong," the Batman said, "but without that witness, the government can't tie Garcia in to that UN plot, and their case against him could go either way. He might still be convicted, but without solid proof, the government would be on shaky ground. So if Specter can eliminate that witness and use terrorist tactics to pressure the government to release Garcia, they may have no choice."

"That's probably true," said Gordon. "But how can you—"

"Hear me out," the Batman said. 'You're going to transfer the witness to another safe house, but you'll let me know the arrangements in advance. Then I will intercept the transfer and abduct the witness."

"No, absolutely not!" said Gordon. "I can't allow it. You'd be kidnapping a federal witness! You'd have not only the police, but the FBI after you as well! Besides, I've got some of my best men handling security. Unless they were all in on it, the risk to you would be too great."

"No, we can't afford to take that chance," the Batman said. "When your men are questioned by the federal authorities—and you may rest assured that they *will* be questioned, and probably asked to take a polygraph—they have to be able to answer truthfully that they had no involvement in this whatsoever. It will mean a risk, of course, but I can see no other way. I'll see to it that none of them are injured, of course, and I'll just have to do my best to make sure that they can't stop me. It will take some careful planning, and the timing will be important, but if I can manage to surprise them, I should be able to pull it off."

Gordon shook his head. "It would never work," he said. "Aside from the risk you would be taking, I'd know about it and I'd be questioned too. And if they asked *me* to take a polygraph and I refused—"

"But you will not refuse," the Batman said. "In fact, you will insist on it."

Gordon stared at him. "You've got to be kidding. How the hell do I beat a polygraph?"

"Simple. You'll be telling the truth. I'll give you a posthypnotic suggestion to forget all about our discussion after you've given me the transfer plans," the Batman said. "I will kidnap the witness, then contact the media and tell them why I've done it. It will make front-page news, and that's exactly what we want."

"But why?"

"From what I know of Specter," said the Batman, "it's easy to infer that he's an assassin who takes pride in his professionalism. His *modus operandi*, his choice of his dramatic name, his signature weapon for his assassinations, his announcement of his intentions to the news media, all point to a high degree of vanity. By kidnapping the witness and then publicly taking credit for it, I'll be throwing down the gauntlet to him. I'm going to bait him, Jim, and try to make him focus his energies on me. It may not stop his acts of terrorism against the people of the city but it might throw him off. It will force him to deal *me* into the equation. In the meantime, I'll be doing everything in my power to find him."

Gordon moistened his lips. "It might work," he said. "But up to this point, you've had a lot of support from the people of this city. This could change all that. You'd be committing a federal crime. That's going past the point of no return."

"Perhaps," the Batman said, "but maybe not. I fully intend to deliver the witness in time for the trial. And with Garcia convicted and Specter apprehended, the FBI might be convinced to drop the charges. I suppose it all depends on whether or not it works, doesn't it? Besides, you have any better ideas?"

Gordon grimaced. "No, I'm sorry to say, I don't." He took a deep breath and let it out slowly. "All right. I just hope you know what you're letting yourself in for. And I hope like hell this works, because you're not going to have much time. We're moving the witness first thing in the morning. Here's how it's going to work..."

Dawn didn't break over Gotham City. It crawled. Like a wary pedestrian out alone at night, the new day seemed to hesitate before it ventured out over the city, as if checking to see whether the coast was clear. The sky was just beginning to turn gray outside when Sergeants Deke Mallory and Rick Rondell stepped out of the stairway door in the basement parking garage and carefully checked the area. They looked like any Gotham City businessmen, except that beneath their coats each man was a walking arsenal.

Each wore a lightweight nylon cordura shoulder holster, Rondell's holding an Austrian semiautomatic constructed of steel and polymer, with a capacity of seventeen 9mm rounds, and Mallory's carrying an American semiauto with a fourteen-round capacity. On the opposite side of their holster rigs, they wore drop pouches for two spare magazines. At their backs, in belt-clip holsters, each man wore a backup pistol. Both men were also expert martial artists, and they each carried a pair of baton nunchuks linked by an unbreakable steel cable, with one baton slipped down inside the sleeves of their jackets and the other hanging loose at their armpits, ready to be grabbed and brought into action instantly. In one hand, Rondell carried a two-way radio. In the other, he held a .45 caliber machine pistol, as did Mallory. They were ready for anything.

Rondell spoke into his radio. "Okay," he said. "It looks clear. We're going to bring up the van. Stand by."

"*Roger,*" came the reply.

He took up position by the elevator, standing with his machine pistol ready, bolt drawn back and round chambered, safety off, while Mallory walked down the center of the parking garage, toward the dark-green Chevy van with the name of a florist painted on the sides. Holding the machine pistol in one hand, Mallory did not go around to the side door, but opened the back door first, unlocking it and swinging it open quickly, then stepping back so that he could cover the inside of the van. Having satisfied himself that it was empty, he signaled Rondell, who came toward him. When Rondell was in position to cover him, Mallory went down to his hands and knees, then turned over onto his back and slid underneath the van, checking out its underside carefully. He then came out and went around to the front. He popped the hood and checked the engine to make sure no one had left any surprises for them during the night. After that, with Rondell still covering him, he carefully checked out the inside of the van. Satisfied, he stuck his head out and nodded to Rondell, who went back toward the elevator.

As Mallory backed the van out of its parking space, Rondell spoke into his radio. "Okay, we're ready down here."

"*Roger. We're on the way.*"

As Mallory pulled the van up to the elevator doors, Rondell stood by, ready with his weapon.

Upstairs, on the fifteenth floor of the luxury security-apartment building, Detective Lieutenant Steve Carman turned to Chambers and said, "Okay, let's get the show on the road."

Detective Sergeant Ross Heintzelman came out of the apartment first, checked the hall in both directions, then started toward the elevator, his .45 semiautomatic held at his side. At this hour, the residents of the building were all still asleep in their beds. None of them were aware that the apartment in the middle of the hall was occupied by a team of FBI agents protecting a federal witness. So far as they knew, the apartment belonged to a large

Gotham City corporation, which used it to house visiting executives.

Carman watched from the door as Heintzelman walked down to the elevator. There was no need to summon it. Rondell and Mallory had already done that before they went down, the long way, by the stairs. The doors had been locked open and the elevator was waiting. It had already been checked out. Rondell had even climbed up through the hatch in the ceiling to make sure there was nothing attached to the outside and that the cable was secure. They were leaving nothing to chance.

"You people seem to know what you're doing," a weary Chambers said to Carman as they prepared to leave.

"We've had a lot of experience with this sort of thing, sir," Lieutenant Carman replied. "The mob's been pretty active in this town. We've had to baby-sit our share of witnesses."

"Well, I don't envy you with this one," Chambers said. "She's a real handful."

Carman smiled wryly. "We've had our share of those as well. Okay, let's get moving."

"Bring her out," said Chambers.

Two of his men came out from the apartment's bedroom, with the government witness between them. She did not look like much of a handful, Carman thought, though he'd already seen enough evidence of her irascible personality to know that this lady was going to be one royal pain in the ass. He wished she could have been a man. With a man, there were certain things you could do, lean on them a little, nothing too heavy, but enough to intimidate them into behaving themselves. With a woman, it was different. You had to use kid gloves, or the next thing you knew, Internal Affairs was all over you.

He took in her sullen, defiant expression as she came out into the living room. He put her age at about twenty-six or twenty-seven. A pretty girl, though she didn't go out of her way to emphasize her natural good looks. Her shoulder-length black hair was worn loose, and she wore almost no makeup. She was dressed in tight, faded jeans, a dull red sweatshirt, a black leather motorcycle jacket, and high-heeled boots. She looked like any other tough little cookie one could find hanging out in the Village rock clubs on any given night. It was hard for Carman to believe that this little girl could single-handedly bring down a powerful man like Desiderio Garcia.

But then, Garcia wasn't so powerful anymore. In his prison coveralls, he looked just like any other con. Take away his snappy uniform, his high-peaked, Nazi-style cap, and all the fruit salad that he wore, and what did you have? A frightened, little fifty-eight-year-old man, sitting alone in maximum security and contemplating a melancholy future as the cellmate of some three-hundred-pound, tattooed lifer name "Mary." It couldn't happen to a nicer guy, thought Carman.

"All right, honey, let's go," he said.

"Don't call me honey, you pig," the witness snapped.

"Sorry, ma'am. No offense meant."

"Yeah, right."

"Would you come with us, please?"

"Have I got any choice?"

"No, ma'am, not really. I'd appreciate it if you stayed

between me and Detective Cruz. It's for your own safety."

"Whatever," she said with a shrug.

"Look," said Chambers, "are you sure you don't want me to—"

"We've already been over that, sir," said Carman. "The commissioner gave us strict instructions."

Chambers sighed. "All right. But for God's sake, be careful. I just hope to hell I'm not going to regret this."

"We'll take good care of her, sir." He nodded to Detective Billy Cruz and they stepped out into the hall, walking quicky toward the elevator as Heintzelman covered them. They got in, and Carman put the elevator key into the lock, releasing the doors.

"Okay, we're on the way down," Carman said into his radio.

"Roger. We're all set here."

The elevator started to descend.

Rondell remained alert while Mallory sat behind the wheel of the van with the motor running. A chime sounded, announcing the arrival of the elevator. The doors slid open. The first thing Rondell saw were the bodies of Carman, Heintzelman, and Cruz sprawled on the floor of the elevator. There was no sign of the witness.

"Jesus Christ!" said Rondell. He quickly stepped into the elevator and bent over the three men, feeling for a pulse, They were alive. He could smell the faint odor of some sort of gas. And the hatch in the ceiling was open.

Mallory came running around the front of the van. *"What the hell happened?"*

"*We've been hit!*" said Rondell. "Quick, give me a leg up!"

Mallory made a cradle with his hands and boosted Rondell up through the ceiling hatch. Rondell crawled out on top of the elevator and looked up. High above him, he could see something moving... the flutter of a cape....

"I don't believe it!" he said. He yelled down through the hatch. "It's the Batman! Take this thing up and get on the horn to Chambers!"

Mallory hit the button for the top floor. Rondell raised his weapon as the elevator started to ascend. They were high above him, rising fast. It looked as if they were floating up the shaft. He figured they were going up on some sort of cable. He couldn't fire for fear of hitting the witness, who was draped over the Batman's shoulder. In the elevator, Mallory was on the two-way, calling Chambers on the fifteenth floor. If the feds could get up to the roof in time, there was a chance that they could cut him off.

The Batman reached the top of the shaft and glanced down. The elevator was rising up to meet him. He could see one man standing on the elevator roof, holding a weapon, but he knew the man wouldn't risk shooting. Gordon's men weren't trigger-happy, and their first concern would be for the witness.

She felt as light as a feather, draped unconscious over his shoulder as he rode up on the automatic hoist. So far, everything had gone off without a hitch, but he knew he'd have to move quickly. By now, they'd have contacted Chambers and his men on the fifteenth floor and they would be rushing for the roof. He had timed everything precisely. He had only minutes left, with no margin for error.

He had landed the Batcopter on the roof, its specially muffled engine barely making any sound at all. It was a sleek, futuristic-looking aircraft, built on the NOTAR design, which meant it had no tail rotor. It substituted a turbine internal blower for the exposed tail-rotor assembly, and it was constructed of graphite, Kevlar, and epoxy-impregnated fiberglass, with graphite-fiber rotors that would allow it to land and take off vertically, like any other chopper. However, at high speed, the rotors were capable of being locked into position, turning the Batcopter into a small, X-wing jet that could approach the speed of sound. It was the ultimate in a light assault aircraft, except that its weapons pods carried only rockets armed with smoke-emitting or nonlethal gas warheads.

The Batman braced himself as he unclipped the cable, which had fully retracted into the motorized spool built into the steel breastplate of the light harness clipped around his chest and shoulders, underneath his cape. He didn't pause to hurl another gas pellet down at the rising elevator; that would have wasted precious seconds. He ignored Rondell and hurried out onto the roof, racing toward the Batcopter with the unconscious woman slung over his shoulder. He strapped her in her seat and hit the starter button. The turbine instantly came to life and the rotors began to spin. He hit the release stud on the breastplate of his chest harness and the thin straps came loose with a click and rapidly retracted into the breastplate and cable-spool housing. He caught it as it dropped away and clipped it to his belt. He quickly checked his instruments, then glanced toward the roof-access door. It was flung open and Chambers and his men came running out onto the roof.

"Close, but no cigar," the Batman said.

The Batcopter rose into the air and quickly receded into the distance, leaving the FBI men standing helpless on the rooftop as the first rosy light of dawn began to touch the sky.

Jim Gordon was an early riser, but he was still asleep in bed when the phone on his bedside table rang. There was a time when he would have quickly snatched it up, hoping to prevent the noise from waking his wife, but for a long time now he had slept alone. He was still on good terms with Barbara, but as was the case with many cops, his marriage had fallen victim to the pressures of the job. The first ring woke him up, but he didn't answer it right away. He glanced at the clock, grunted with irritation, and picked the phone up on the third ring.

"This had better be important," he growled into the mouthpiece.

"Your men just lost my witness," Chambers said with cold fury. "That important enough for you?"

Gordon instantly sat up in bed. "*What?*"

"They didn't have her in custody five minutes before they blew it," Chambers said. "Your friend the Batman's got her. You remember, the one you told me not to worry about?"

Gordon was stunned. He remembered nothing of the plan he had concocted with the Batman. After they had discussed the details of the plan, the Batman had put him under and given him a posthypnotic suggestion. Then he had driven home and gone to bed. At two o'clock in the morning, his phone rang and he answered it. He heard the Batman speak the words "The Songbird has flown." He repeated what he heard, hung up the phone, and went to sleep. He woke up with no memory of their meeting.

"Gordon? *Gordon!*"

"Yes I—I'm here," said Gordon, still shaken by what he'd just heard. He rubbed his forehead. He felt dazed.

"What the hell do we do *now?*" asked Chambers.

"Look," said Gordon, "are you sure it was the Batman? I mean, there couldn't be a mistake?"

"I saw him with my own damn eyes," said Chambers. "He used some kind of gas to knock out your men while they were on their way down in the elevator, then he grabbed the witness and went up the shaft on some kind of motorized cable hoist. He had a goddamn helicopter on the roof, looked like something out of a science-fiction movie. Took off like a rocket and hardly made a sound. I was standing right there when it happened."

"I don't understand," said Gordon. "Why would he do that?"

"*Why?*" said Chambers. "Why do you think? He was bought off. What I want to know is *how* he did it. How the hell did he *know?* How did he find out where we had the witness? How did he find out she was being transferred this morning?"

"I . . . I have no idea," Gordon said. "I still can't believe it. Was anyone hurt?"

"No, he pulled the whole thing off like clockwork. The bastard made it look easy. And I'm left here with my ass hanging out in the wind. I suggest you get down to your office right away. It's about to hit the fan, and we're both going to have some hard questions to answer."

"Yes, of course. I'll be right there," said Gordon.

"One more thing," Chambers said. "There's going to be a full investigation. This wasn't a coincidence, not by a long shot. Somebody tipped off the Batman, and I intend to find out who it was. I'm going to have my head handed to me for this, and I'll be damned if I'm going to take the rap alone."

He slammed the phone down before Gordon could respond.

She started to come to in the Batcopter, and, for a moment, she was disoriented. She tried to move forward, but found herself restrained by a safety strap across her chest.

"What the hell . . . ?" she mumbled, still slightly groggy from the effects of the knockout gas.

"Please remain still," said a deep and resonant voice close beside her. "There is no cause for alarm. You are in safe hands, I assure you."

She jerked, startled, and in a rapid strobe-flash of jarring images and sense impressions, suddenly realized that she was in some sort of aircraft flying high above the clouds. And sitting in the seat beside her was . . .

"*The Batman!*"

He glanced at her briefly and nodded. "Yes, ma'am. Please don't be alarmed. I mean you no harm."

"What . . . what *happened?* How did I . . . where are you *taking* me?"

"To a place of safekeeping," he replied. "The rest of your questions will have to wait awhile, I'm afraid. We're about to descend. Please keep your seat belt fastened."

They were descending into a heavy cloud bank. Within seconds, she could see nothing through the cockpit glass except the swirling cloud mist. They were dropping fast, straight down. Too fast, it seemed to her, much too fast, but the Batman seemed perfectly calm and in control as he piloted the craft. Suddenly, the mist was gone and darkness closed in all around them. Complete and utter darkness. She felt a very slight jar as the skids touched down. The Batman worked several controls on the console, and she heard the descending whine of the turbine as the rotors above slowed and finally stopped, though in the darkness, she couldn't even see them. She couldn't see a thing except the soft glow of the instruments in the cockpit.

"You may release your seat belt now," the Batman said.

She fumbled with the belt but couldn't get it undone. She still felt slightly groggy. Then, suddenly, the lights came on. She gasped. They were in some sort of hangar; it seemed to be a hangar carved from solid rock, with walls that sloped upward to a peak, where two heavy steel doors, like giant hatch covers, concealed the entryway. Floodlights had been mounted on the inside of the hangar, up near the ceiling, and about midway up the walls. She realized, with a start, that the helicopter was moving.

They were on some sort of giant turntable that was revolving slowly, giving her a full view of the inside of the hangar. There were banks of instruments along the walls, and sheet steel, and heavy tools and ramps and scaffolding and all the sorts of things one could expect to find inside the hangars of any large commercial airline.

But as they revolved, she saw one thing that could *not* be found inside any major airline's hangars—the Batplane.

She'd heard of it, but she had never actually seen it. And it was truly an impressive sight. She knew a little bit about airplanes, having flown in them often enough, and she realized that this was no ordinary aircraft. It was as unique as the helicopter that had brought her here. The Batplane was sleek, compact and jet black, designed for vertical takeoff and landing, like the British Harrier jets. It was obviously built for speed. Supersonic speed. Its lines made her think of a cross between a miniature Stealth bomber and an F-18. Its construction appeared almost seamless, smooth with no harsh angles, the cockpit incorporated into the sweep of the wings for maximum aerodynamic efficiency. It made her think of a giant boomerang, or a delta wing. The latest Air Force fighter jets looked like antiques compared to it.

The turntable stopped revolving, and she watched with fascination as some kind of robotic cart shuttled out toward them. The Batman seemed to be controlling it from inside the cockpit. It was built low to the ground, and as it scooted underneath the copter she heard a couple of metallic clicks as something underneath locked into position. The copter rose about a foot, as if on a lift, and then moved forward. She realized the cart was slowly trundling it off the turntable. A moment later, the cart stopped and lowered the Batcopter to the hangar floor.

"We can get out now," said the Batman. "Allow me...."

He reached over and, with a quick flick of his finger,

released the lock on her seat belt. He opened the hatch and got out, then helped her down.

"Wow," she said, looking around with astonishment. "Is this the Batcave?"

"Well, no, not really," replied the Batman. "This is only the hangar. The Batcave is directly below us. If you'll follow me, please?"

He led her over to a spot on the floor near the center of the hangar, just to the side of the giant turntable. There was nothing there except a small control panel, mounted on a slender metal pole, about waist high.

"Are you nervous about heights?" the Batman asked incongruously as he rested his hand on the control panel.

"Huh?"

"You may wish to take my arm," he said, offering it to her.

"Why?"

He pushed a button on the control panel, and they started to descend. Suddenly, she found herself standing by his side on a round section of floor no more than four feet in diameter, with nothing around them except empty space. Instinctively, she grabbed his arm for support.

They were descending on some sort of hydraulic lift into a huge cavern, with large stalactites hanging from the ceiling and veins of shimmering crystal in the walls. It was like entering another world. She tensed as something flew past them and she heard the sound of chittering.

"Don't mind my little friends," the Batman said. "They won't harm you."

As she held on to him, she could not help being aware of the huge, rock-hard muscles of his upper arm. His biceps were the size of softballs, and his triceps were huge, their horseshoe shape sharply defined. But her attention was captured by the cavern they were descending into. She had never seen anything like it. It looked like a cross between something out of a science-fiction thriller and a secret underground military base.

Portions of the cavern floor had been finished with what she first thought was concrete but soon realized was some sort of ultrasmooth, epoxy resin. Other portions of the cavern floor were left natural, with rock outcroppings and stone formations jutting out. As they descended, she saw a small fleet of Batmobiles, at least a dozen of them, looking like exhibits in a custom car show, from the earliest model with its winglike fins and bat's-head front grill, to the latest model, smaller and more aerodynamically shaped, like something designed for a production racing team. The hood on one of the vehicles was open, revealing a sophisticated engine that was in the process of being overhauled. The overall effect was as if someone had taken the war room at NORAD and dropped it into a huge cavern. The elevator platform stopped.

"Welcome to the Batcave," said the Batman.

CHAPTER
SIX

IT was lunchtime, and the streets were crowded. It was one of the busiest times of the day for many stores in the city, as people on their lunch break shopped or simply browsed after grabbing a quick salad at their favorite restaurant. The large, multistoried Barrington's department store was one of the most fashionable retail outlets in the city; it had merchandise catering to every taste and budget, from off-the-rack clothing to designer fashions, from relatively inexpensive perfumes to pricey fragrances named after celebrities. It was Friday, and the store was crowded as consumers spent their paychecks or simply window-shopped.

So when the explosion ripped through the department store at half past twelve, it took a devastating toll in human lives.

Among the spectators crowding the sidewalk beyond the police barricades as the fire department fought the blaze, a tall, good-looking, pale man with snow-white hair and sharply chiseled features stood calmly smoking a French cigarette. He finished it and stubbed it out beneath the toe of his handmade Italian shoe, then turned and walked briskly down the block until he came to a telephone booth near the corner. He deposited a quarter and quickly dialed a number.

"Newsroom," a voice on the other end answered.

"I would like to speak to Enrique Vasquez, please."

"May I ask who's calling, sir?"

"This is Specter. If he's not on the line within twenty seconds, I am hanging up."

"One moment, please..."

Vasquez picked up the phone in ten seconds flat.

"Enrique Vasquez," he said. "Specter? Is that you?"

"Good afternoon, Mr. Vasquez. I have just bombed Barrington's department store. This should demonstrate the seriousness of my intent. Tell the people of Gotham City that this is only the beginning. For every day that General Garcia remains in custody, there will be another incident... and more people will die. I will be in touch."

He hung up before Vasquez could ask him any questions, then calmly walked away.

For Jim Gordon, the day had started early, with the angry phone call from Chambers, and it kept on going downhill from there. The weary and frustrated detectives whom he had assigned to the government's witness had been steadily grilled by Chambers and his men, as well as by Internal Affairs, for hours on end. Every one of them had volunteered to take a polygraph, and every one of them had passed. Gordon himself had insisted on taking a polygraph examination, along with his men, and he had passed as well. Chambers was at his wits' end.

He sat slumped in the chair in Gordon's office, chain-smoking, his tie loosened and the top two buttons of his rumpled shirt undone, the circles around his eyes looking deeper and darker, his hair unkempt from the way he kept running his hand through it in exasperation.

"I can't understand it," he said wearily. "We repeated the tests twice and everybody passed. Nobody except those men and you knew about the transfer. None of them talked to anybody else about it. None of *my* men talked. I put 'em all on the machine myself. And *I* sure as hell didn't spill the beans to anybody. So how in God's name did the Batman *know*?"

Gordon sighed heavily. "The Batman has a way of knowing and doing things that often seem completely inexplicable."

"Yeah? What is he, a mind reader? He got a tap on your phone?" Chambers suddenly snapped his fingers. "Damn it! That's gotta be it! He's got this office bugged!"

"I'm sorry to disappoint you," Gordon replied, "but that's *not* it. I have this office swept for surveillance devices every day as a matter of routine. You're not the only one who's paranoid, you know."

Chambers grimaced. "Look, no offense, but you mind if I have my people do their own sweep?"

"Help yourself," said Gordon. "But you won't find anything, I can promise you that."

There was a knock at the door.

"Come in," said Gordon.

"Commissioner?" said Sergeant Capiletti. "Sir, it's almost one o'clock, and I know you've been in since five

A.M. You haven't had a thing to eat, and I don't think Mr. Chambers has, either. I was wondering if I couldn't send out for something?"

"I could use a sandwich," Gordon said wearily. "Chambers?"

"Hell, I couldn't eat a bite," said Chambers with a grimace. "My stomach is in knots. I'm not sure I could keep anything down. Just black coffee, Capiletti. Lots of it. And thanks."

"What I don't understand is why he did it," Gordon said, thinking out loud. "The Batman has always cooperated with the police before."

"Like I told you, Commissioner," said Chambers, "he must've been bought off. We'll probably find her floating facedown in the East River."

Gordon shook his head. "No, I could never believe that."

"Jesus Christ, you're *still* defending him?" Chambers said with disbelief.

"He *must* have had a reason," Gordon said. "No matter what you think, the Batman's not a killer. He abducted the witness, but he did it without harming anyone. And he easily could have. No, I just can't believe the Batman could have been bought off by anyone. He's not a criminal."

"He's a fruitcake vigilante, Gordon," said Chambers. "Maybe you should wake up and smell the coffee."

The phone on Gordon's desk rang, and he picked it up. As he listened, the color drained from his face. "Oh, my God," he said.

"What is it?" Chambers asked.

Gordon hung up the phone. "Specter just bombed

Barrington's. News crews are on the scene already." He got up, went over to the TV set atop the file cabinet, and turned it on.

The picture on the screen was a scene of carnage and devastation. Flames licked from the windows of Barrington's department store as fire fighters struggled to bring the conflagration under control. Police cars and ambulances were arriving with sirens blaring; people milled about on the sidewalks, trying to get a better view. It was utter chaos.

"Repeating once more, this is a special report, coming to you live from Barrington's department store, the site of a devastating explosion that occurred at approximately twelve-thirty this afternoon. Witnesses report a huge, concussive blast that came from within the building, and speculation at this point is that it was a bomb, perhaps more than one, although we cannot as yet confirm that. At this point, three companies of Gotham City's fire department have responded to the alarm. It is impossible right now to determine how many people have been killed or injured, but the number is certainly significant. Fire fighters have been bringing bodies out, and many more are undoubtedly still inside. We don't know at this point if any survivors are trapped inside the building, but standing here and looking at this awful scene, it seems impossible to believe that anyone could still be alive in there. We have, at this point—"

"John," broke in the anchorman, "we've just received an update. It seems we have someone claiming responsibility for the bombing. We're going to cut away from you for a moment. Please stand by."

The reporter nodded, holding a hand to his headset,

and then once more spoke into the mike. "Right, Tom, go ahead."

"As I've just said," the anchorman repeated, "for those of you just tuning in, there's been an explosion at Barrington's department store, apparently a bomb, and we've just received word that someone has contacted us to take credit for this dreadful act. We go now to Enrique Vasquez, in the newsroom. Enrique, are you there?"

The camera cut to Vasquez, in his shirt sleeves, his tie undone, wearing a headset and holding a mike and looking haggard. "Tom, just moments ago, I received a call here in the newsroom from a man identifying himself as Specter and claiming responsibility for the bombing. Now, I spoke to Specter once before, and I recognized his voice. It was that same, cultured-sounding, European accent. And he asked for me by name."

"Jesus Christ," said Chambers.

"Specter told me," Vasquez continued, holding up a slip of paper, "and I quote, 'I have just bombed Barrington's department store. This should demonstrate the seriousness of my intent. Tell the people of Gotham City that this is only the beginning. For every day that General Garcia remains in custody, there will be another incident and more people will die. I will be in touch.' And then he abruptly hung up."

"Enrique," said the anchorman, "have the police been notified of this communication?"

"I assume they're hearing it now, Tom," Vasquez replied. "It only just happened, as I've said, and I will be giving them a written copy of the text of this communication as soon as I can. But it appears as if Specter has made good on his threat against the people of this city, and I can only hope that Commissioner James Gordon is listening. He told me the other day, when I informed him of Specter's first communication, his threat to commit terrorist acts against the people of Gotham City, that he doesn't deal in speculation, only in facts. Well, it's a fact now, Commissioner, a horrible, tragic fact, and from what Specter said, we can only look forward with dread to more of the same.''

"Thank you very much, Mr. Vasquez," Gordon said through gritted teeth.

"Enrique," said the anchorman, "as I recall the message you just read, Specter said that he would be 'in touch.' What do you suppose that means?"

"Tom, at this point I really don't know," Vasquez replied. "I can only speculate as to what he meant by that. He hung up before I could ask him any questions, and from the background noise—I distinctly heard some screams—I assume that he was calling from a public phone near the scene of the explosion. It may be that he meant the city would be hearing from him again, the way we've 'heard' from him today, through this savage act of terror, or perhaps he meant that he would be in touch with me, personally. I don't know, but somehow that was the impression that I got, although as I've already said, that's only speculation on my part at this point. However, if that is the case, and for some reason Specter has selected *me* to be his messenger of doom, then God knows, Tom, I didn't ask for this, but it's my responsibility as a journalist and as a citizen to pass on what he communicates to me, and much as I wish I could, I can't turn my back on it."

"Turn his back on it, hell," said Gordon with disgust.

"He's loving every minute of this." He angrily turned off the set and picked up his phone. "Get on the horn," he said, "and tell Vasquez I want to see him in my office *now* or I'll bust him for withholding evidence." He slammed the phone down. "Son of a ..." He looked up at Chambers. "What the hell do we do now?"

Chambers shook his head helplessly. "I don't know. We pull out all the stops and try to catch the bastard before he kills any more people. How many more officers can you put on the task force?"

"I'll give you all the people I can," said Gordon.

"I'm not sure how much good it's going to do," said Chambers. "There's going to be a lot of pressure on us now to knuckle under to his demands and put Garcia on that plane to Cuba. And without our star witness, I'm not sure we have much of a case. We may not have any choice."

Gordon's phone rang. He picked it up. "Gordon," he said. He listened for a moment. "Yes, sir... Yes, Mr. Mayor, I know, I just saw it on the news... We're doing all we can... No, sir, I don't really know, that's not my jurisdiction. I guess you'll have to speak to the federal authorities about that... Yes, sir... Yes, sir, I will... Yes, sir, I fully understand. I share your concern... Right."

He hung up the phone. "Well," he said to Chambers with a sigh, "it's started."

The Batman sat in the glass-walled, central control room of the Batcave, watching the special coverage of the bombing with a stricken expression on his face. All those people... Specter had simply wiped them off the face of the earth as casually as if he had swatted a fly.

The Batman's mind was tormented by the images he *hadn't* seen on the television news coverage, images that were just as clearly, just as vividly, just as horribly visible to him as if he'd been there himself. Images of businessmen using the free time of their lunch break to buy anniversary presents for their wives. Young clerks and college boys and record-store salesmen buying something for their girlfriends for that special thank-God-it's-Friday-night date. Secretaries and bank employees and saleswoman picking out that new dress they'd been saving up for, or just browsing with girlfriends after an inexpensive lunch. Housewives taking advantage of a sale, trying to keep their children from running off down between the aisles... The children. My God, the children...

He thought of the devastating explosion tearing them apart, and he thought of those who hadn't been killed outright but who were trapped, torn and bleeding, underneath the wreckage as the flames cooked them alive... He sat, eyes staring, numb with horror, an unbearable tightness in his chest as he imagined, as he *felt*, all that human agony, and a single tear welled up and dripped down the outside of his cowl. Without realizing it, he had started moving in his chair, rocking slowly back and forth, in an unconscious regression to the same, shock-induced motions he had made when, as a child, he had knelt over the bodies of his parents, knelt in the blood of his father and his mother, stunned into insensibility at their lives' being so suddenly and brutally snuffed out. What kind of man could *do* something like this?

He had spent most of the morning with the girl. It was

hard for him to think of her as a woman, though at twenty-seven, she most certainly was that. She seemed so young in many ways, years younger than she really was, but in other ways years older. At first she had seemed frightened and bewildered, like a lost child, but after he explained to her why he had abducted her from the police, and after she began to realize that she truly had nothing to fear from him, she had reverted to a street-smart sort of toughness, a rude defiance marked by an abrasive and hard-edged personality that had obviously been cultivated carefully to conceal the vulnerability within.

He might have bought it had he not seen her earlier reactions when she first came to inside the Batcopter and then saw the interior of the Batcave. The way she had clutched at him when the elevator descended from the hangar, the way her eyes had gone wide with fright and uncertainty, her revealing body language... it all told him that despite the outward pose of toughness she'd adopted, inside there was a frightened little girl who'd somehow had her childhood stolen from her.

He'd seen it all before, more times than he cared to count. He'd seen it in the eyes of runaways who'd fled lives of abuse and misery, children whose harsh and uncertain life in the streets seemed infinitely preferable to what they had experienced at home. Occasionally, if they were caught in time, it was possible to save them. If someone cared enough, if someone got to them soon enough, and took them to someone like Dr. Leslie Thompkins, who could provide shelter and education and activities to occupy their time and, most importantly, the caring and support that would help them find a sense of self-worth and convince them to respect themselves, prove to them that *life* was infinitely preferable to mere existence, then maybe, just maybe, they could have the opportunity to take advantage of something few people ever get—a second chance.

But that time in which they could still be reached was no more than a tiny window of opportunity, and when it closed, almost without exception it could never again be opened. The cruel realities of life in the streets of the big city, where your body was no more than a cheap commodity to be used up and discarded, were like the deadly glance of the Medusa. They turned your heart to stone. And once that window closed, cutting them off forever from the children they had been, they metamorphosed into feral creatures of the night.

They became jaded hookers who allowed their youthful bodies to be used for the ephemeral gratification of their customers, to whom impersonal and sleazy sex had become a shallow, empty substitute for love. They became junkies who would beg or steal or maim or even kill to pacify, if only for a few brief hours, that relentless evil monkey on their backs, using drugs to dull their senses, to seek a temporary oblivion that would all too soon become permanent. They became hopeless alcoholics, empty vessels to be filled with the dregs of discarded whiskey bottles that they found in filthy Dumpsters, and they slept in doorways and on the subway gratings and on the sidewalks in pools of their own urine, their humanity forever lost. They became the walking dead.

And as frightening and heartbreaking as the victims were, there were the survivors, who instead of taking out the pain of their existence on themselves, became the predators who preyed upon the citizenry. They became the habitual offenders, the hardened criminals, the murderers and rapists and armed robbers and loan sharks and leg-breakers and muggers and organized-crime hit men, people who were utterly devoid of a conscience, who cared nothing for the pain of others, for they simply could not feel or understand it. Or they simply didn't care. *They* were beyond reach.

It could be argued that society had done it to them, or it could be argued that they had allowed their values to be corrupted by selfishness and greed. Or that they'd simply been "born bad," and in some cases, as with sociopaths, that was literally true. However, one thing could not be argued. At some point in their lives, they had all been somebody's child. Those who had been loved and cared for, those whose needs were seen to, those who had been nurtured and who knew the difference between right and wrong and made the wrong choice by virtue of expediency, those were not hard to blame. But what of those who had been born unwanted, or abandoned, or abused? What of those who had never known the joy of childish laughter, who had been denied parental love, or who, quite simply, due to circumstances that occurred more and more often in a too-crowded and too-uncaring world, had simply never had a chance? For those, it was possible to bleed.

The Batman knew little of this girl, this young woman, who now occupied a bedroom in the finished section of the Batcave. He knew only her name. Rachel. Rachel Morrison, or "Ray," as she wanted to be called, seeking a masculine toughness even in her name, as if to deny her suburban, middle-class, WASP origins. What the

Batman knew about her was the little he had learned from Gordon, who had seen her file. She had been born in Darien, Connecticut, the daughter of a well-to-do stockbroker and his wife, who had divorced when she was only four, a traumatic experience for any child, but especially one so young. The stockbroker ex-husband had been too quick for the lawyers. He had transferred and liquidated all his assets, walked on the mortgage, and dropped out of sight. So there was no alimony and no child support. Her mother had moved to a small apartment in New York City and taken a job as stockworker in a large department store. It hadn't paid much, nowhere near enough for a decent apartment and everything they needed. Life was a struggle, made all the more painful when Rachel's mother learned that her daughter had been steadily abused over a period of months by the young woman she had taken in to baby-sit her.

The troubled girl had grown up and gone to school, getting good grades but being branded early as a rebellious troublemaker and a loner. She went to college at the State University, more to please her mother than out of any desire of her own, and it was there that she attended a controversial lecture by a representative of the PLO. The Palestinian's appearance was picketed and he was heckled and booed by the audience, which was perhaps what first aroused the young girl's sympathy. She spoke to him afterward, and they met several times thereafter, and he told her about the plight of the Palestinian people. Apparently, they soon became lovers. It led to a trip abroad, where she could see and experience firsthand the things he had described to her, and either through him, or through some of his more radical friends, Rachel soon became involved in the more militant branch of Arafat's organization.

She first became a fanatic for a cause, and then the means became the cause, and she was soon linked to a number of terrorist organizations who pursued activities not only in Israel, but in West Germany, Italy, Great Britain, and France. At some point, she attended a training camp in Latin America operated under the auspices of General Desiderio Garcia, who was known to have a weakness for young women. She became his mistress, and he apparently had not been able to resist bragging in bed about his exploits and his deals, his connections with foreign intelligence organizations, terrorist groups, and the infamous Macro drug cartel.

She lived in pampered luxury, the mistress of a wealthy and powerful dictator, a man who was cruel and abusive, and who practiced occult rites, and who treated his people as if they were nothing more than chattel. At some point, something happened, some straw that broke the camel's back, and Rachel had had enough. While out on a shopping expedition, she gave the slip to her guards and sought asylum in the American embassy. In return for a trip back home, full immunity, and the promise of a new beginning, she agreed to testify against Garcia.

Garcia and whoever was behind him—undoubtedly the powerful Macro cartel, who stood to lose a lot if Garcia started talking—knew there was a witness, but they did not know that it was Rachel. An elaborate subterfuge had been played out to safeguard her identity. The CIA had concocted a phony kidnap plot, complete with a ransom note delivered to Garcia, along with some of Rachel's jewelry and personal possessions, and as they had expected,

Garcia had completely disregarded it. He had simply found himself another mistress, one that was much younger.

The CIA had told Rachel she was safe. But the fact was, she would never be safe, not until Garcia was permanently behind bars and the Macro cartel put out of business. She simply knew too much. The Macros wanted Garcia out of jail, and they wanted the government witness against him eliminated. Even if Garcia went down, as he most certainly would, the damage Rachel could do to the Macros would ensure a powerful vendetta against her for the rest of her life. She would always be looking over her shoulder. No one should have to live with that.

He had been talking with her, explaining things, telling her that all her comforts would be seen to and that she would not have to spend all her time confined to that one room, but that she would have free run of the Batcave so long as she was escorted by either Alfred or himself—though of course he had not used Alfred's name, and Alfred would disguised himself with a wig, a fake beard, and latex facial applicances so that she would never be able to recognize him—when Alfred had called down to him on the special intercom from upstairs, telling him to turn on the news at once.

As the Batman watched the results of Specter's handiwork, emotions stormed within him: grief for the helpless victims, horror for the incredible callousness and unspeakable brutality of such an act, and cold, hard rage and hatred for the killer who called himself Specter. He resolved that he would move heaven and earth to find this remorseless mass murderer and bring him to justice. He would exorcise this Specter even if it cost him all his fortune and took every waking hour of the remainder of his life. If he ever felt the urge to kill, he came close to feeling it now, but that was something he could never do. That way lay damnation; if he succumbed to that temptation, no matter how well justified it seemed to be, he would become the same as those he hunted. The same, God help him, as Joe Chill, his parents' killer. Sensei Sato had been right. The act of killing was inconceivable to him. Besides, death was too good for a man like Specter. Life in prison, in maximum security, in a tiny cell all by himself, where he could contemplate the consequences of his crimes, was the very least that he deserved. If there really was a hell, then Specter had more than earned his passage across the River Styx. And if there was any justice in the universe, he would burn forever.

The Batman turned to Alfred. "Have you got the camera ready?" he asked.

"Yes, sir," Alfred said, holding the small video recorder. "We can begin whenever you are ready."

"Let's take it outside," the Batman said. "We'll shoot against the rock formation. A properly dark background for my message to Specter. I want to do it now, while I still feel all this rage burning up my gut. I want him to see it, *feel* it, and know that nothing on this earth will stop me from finding him!"

As always when he came back to the apartment in the Village, he went by a circuitous route to make sure he wasn't being followed. Then he didn't go directly into the building, but carefully observed the area and circled the block, twice, taking note of the vehicles on the street and the windows and rooftops of the surrounding buildings. Caution had, over the years, become second nature with him. He never forgot himself and he never relaxed his guard for an instant. He was a pro, and he took great satisfaction in his competency. He left nothing to chance. Ever.

Once inside the front door of the building, he stood still for a moment and listened carefully, his every sense alert. A crying child down the hall. A couple arguing somewhere upstairs. A radio playing rock music. Nothing out of the ordinary. Nothing felt wrong. Just the same, he proceeded up the stairs cautiously, conscious of the reassuring weight of the Grizzly in his special breakfront shoulder holster. His jacket had been specially tailored to prevent any telltale bulges, and the coat he wore over it made the weapon impossible to spot. But it was there, with the silencer screwed into place, ready in case of trouble. As was the second apartment he had subletted on the other side of town, just in case this one was compromised. It was all part of the overhead, and he did not mind the added expense. He was getting paid extremely well for his work, and the extra margin of safety was well worth it.

He reached his floor and paused before entering the hallway. Listening. Smelling. Extending his almost preternatural awareness out into the corridor. Years of stalking, and of being stalked, had honed his senses to an animal instinct, so that things most people did not, could not even notice, because of the casual and secure way in which they went about their lives, did not escape him. The elderly couple down the hall were cooking Chinese food again. The young secretary who spent almost every night out cruising the bars, looking for Mr. Right, had only recently arrived home. He could still smell the faint trace of her lilac perfume in the hall. She had checked him out early on, with an almost predatory aggression, but he had avoided her easily enough by assuming certain mannerisms, and she quickly lost interest. Everything seemed normal.

He approached the door of his apartment and checked for signs that anyone might have been inside. The three tiny strips of filament tape he had placed around the door—one at the top, one at the bottom, and one along the side, small enough and thin enough to be invisible unless one knew exactly where to look—were still in place. Satisfied, he unlocked the door and entered.

Once inside, he removed his coat and jacket and lit up a cigarette. It was not a common brand, but French, unfiltered, available here at inflated prices only in tobacconist shops. He could not abide American cigarettes, with all their additives that supposedly enhanced the flavor but actually did nothing for the taste and only made the cigarettes burn faster. French cigarettes contained nothing but tobacco, which was why their taste was harsh to American palates, which were accustomed to the grosser things in life, such as their fast-food hamburgers and greasy french fries, their syrupy soft drinks and their watered down beer. Only the British, he thought, ate worse food than Americans.

He brushed back his thick white hair and loosened his silk tie. He left the shoulder holster on. Out of long habit, he was never without a weapon close at hand, not even when he slept. His only concession to comfort was to loosen his tie and remove the lightweight nylon sheath from beneath his left sleeve. It fastened around his forearm with Velcro straps and held a shortened, custom-made version of the Fairburn-Sykes commando knife, a triangular-shaped stiletto that came to a sharp point, with both sides of the blade honed to razor sharpness.

He put on the teakettle and prepared the pot, carefully measuring out the loose Indian tea. Then he washed his hands and splashed some water on his face, turned on the television, and settled down to read the paper while he waited for the water to boil. Some inane afternoon talk show was on, with the host simpering and sprinkling his questions with sly innuendo as he interviewed a group of male strippers. With a grimace of distaste, he turned down the volume.

He noticed with satisfaction that the Garcia case, and especially his announced threat, were still getting a lot of play in the headlines. Nowhere near as much play as it was going to get now, he thought, smiling to himself. The teakettle started whistling, and he went back into the kitchen to make the tea. By the time he returned, the talk show had ended and the evening news was coming on. He turned up the volume.

"Good evening, this is Roger Greeley, and here is tonight's news. Downtown Gotham City was the scene of carnage and destruction earlier today when a bomb ripped through Barrington's department store shortly after noon. For further details, we go to Connie Williams...."

He watched the taped footage and listened to the updated information, heard the fire chief interviewed, as well as the senior police officer on the scene. There were comments from individual fire fighters, and from paramedics, as well as from a number of witnesses to the explosion. There were interviews with people waiting to find out if their loved ones had been inside the store when the bomb went off. The American news media loved to wallow in disaster. It was perfect, he thought, absolutely perfect.

Then came the press conference with Enrique Vasquez, playing the dedicated martyr in his supposedly unwanted role as Specter's messenger, promising full cooperation with the police and federal authorities, insisting that he was not afraid, that he had a job to do, a serious responsibility, and so forth, all the while milking the attention for all that it was worth. Oh, yes, Vasquez was the perfect cat's-paw, the ideal choice to ensure maximum publicity. But what came next took him by surprise.

"Shortly before we went on the air tonight," the anchorman announced, "we received a videotape cassette, anonymously delivered to our reception desk downstairs. The envelope was marked to our attention, but had no other markings on it except one—the stylized image of a bat, the symbol of the Batman. Needless to say, its contents were intriguing. We will play that tape for you now."

Specter sat forward in his chair as the image of the Batman, taped in close-up against a dark and rocky background, came on the screen.

"This is the Batman. Early this morning, I abducted the government witness against General Garcia from the authorities. That witness is now in my personal custody, safe and unharmed inside the Batcave. I did it to make certain that the witness *remained* safe and unharmed, and able to testify against General Garcia at his upcoming trial. I want to reassure the authorities that at the proper time and place, I will produce the witness, but until that time, there is no place safer than the Batcave. I am immune to public and political pressure, and to pressure from Garcia's lawyers and the media. The witness will remain in my protective custody, and the degenerate and psychopathic murderer who calls himself 'Specter' will be frustrated in his efforts to fulfill his contract. On that, you have my solemn pledge.

"I have only one other thing to add. I know that Specter will be watching this, just as a sick pyromaniac cannot help but watch the flames with fascination, and it is to him that I address these words."

The camera came in tighter, until the Batman's masked face filled the screen.

"You style yourself as a 'professional,' an expert in a lethal craft, but what you have done today was not a job of craftsmanship, but butchery. You have demonstrated that you are no more than a common thug, no different from a demented arsonist or a mad bomber who strikes indiscriminately and at a cowardly distance. It does not take a 'professional' to kill helpless women and children. There is no 'craft' in striking at a man when you cannot even face him. You are no different from countless terrorists before you, cowardly little men who hatched their plots in secret and committed wanton acts of murder and destruction out of some sick, grandiose delusion that they were struggling for a cause and making a difference in the world. You are not different. You are not superior. You are merely another butcher in a long line of sick and twisted little men, acting out their insane compulsions to make up for their own inadequacy. And like the insect that you are, you must be stepped on.

"Know this. Whoever you are, *wherever* you are, I will find you. I will drag you out into the light of day, out from beneath whatever rock you're hiding under, and I will deliver you up to the authorities so that you may spend the rest of your miserable, natural life inside a cell. I am the exorcist who will rid this city of you, Specter. You may run, like the cowardly assassin that you are, but there is no place on this earth where you can hide!"

The tape ended and the camera cut back to the anchorman. "We have learned that the police, as well as all the networks, have received a copy of this tape. The Batman's message is unmistakable. The gauntlet has been thrown. When reached for comment, Police Commissioner James Gordon—"

The screen exploded as the thrown teapot struck it with full force, sending sparks and smoke and shards of glass and ceramic flying in all directions. Specter was livid with fury. To be insulted on national television by some clown in a masquerade costume, some melodramatic fool who dared to interfere with him. He stood there, breathing heavily, his fists clenching and unclenching, staring at the ruined television set as if he could still see the Batman's face.

"So," he said, struggling to compose himself, "I am an insect to be stepped on, am I? Well, we shall see, my costumed friend, which of us shall be exterminated!"

He threw on his coat and hurried out of the apartment, down to the public phone booth at the corner. He deposited a coin and quickly punched out the number of the newsroom. This time, he didn't bother asking for Enrique Vasquez. When the call was answered, he merely said,

"This is Specter. Tell the Batman that tomorrow, there will be not one, but *two* more demonstrations, one for General Garcia, and one especially for him. Tell him that Specter has picked up the gauntlet."

He slammed down the receiver, then ripped it from its cord and hurled it out into the street. Before he was through, he would have the people of this city clamoring for Garcia's release. And howling for the Batman's head. Which he would gladly give to them, wrapped up in a box and delivered to the office of Commissioner James Gordon.

CHAPTER
SEVEN

It was one place where the reporters could not get at them because the clientele would make certain they were kept at bay. McTaggert's was a cop bar, a couple of blocks away from police headquarters, located in the basement of an elegant old brownstone. There were no hanging ferns here, and no nouvelle cuisine, just an old bar steeped with character, where the most common drink was whiskey with a beer back and the jukebox played old songs by Tormé, Bennett, and Sinatra. Commissioner James Gordon and FBI agent Reese Chambers were hunkered down in a dark booth in the back corner, with a pitcher of beer between them and several empty shot glasses of whiskey lined up on the table like a row of toy soldiers.

"Well," said Chambers, "it looks like your friend, the Batman, has only made things worse."

A short while ago, they had received a phone call from

the newsroom and learned of Specter's ominous acceptance of the challenge.

"The Batman is not responsible for what Specter does, Reese," said Gordon. "He's only trying to help. And believe me, help is something we need very badly right now."

"Yeah, sure," said Chambers wryly. "Imagine what would happen if every citizen took it in his head that the Bureau and the cops couldn't get the job done by themselves and needed help. We'd have a goddamned war zone out there."

"The Batman is not just any citizen," said Gordon. "He is a very highly trained and very capable individual, with extensive resources at his command. And no matter what you think, Reese, he *is* on our side."

Chambers sighed. "I'll take your word for it that he means well. But now we haven't got our witness, and despite his promise to deliver her at the proper time and place, we have no guarantee that he will do that, or that he can keep her safe."

"Nobody knows where the Batcave is," said Gordon. "Specter will never be able to find it. And even if he does manage to find it somehow, the Batman will be waiting for him."

Chambers stared at him contemplatively. "The way you speak about him, Jim, you'd think you really knew the guy. You do, don't you?"

Gordon shook his head. "I don't know who the Batman is. And that's the honest truth."

"I believe you," Chambers said, "but that's not the answer to the question I asked. Look, you and I are in this thing together. We've got both our asses in the wringer. Off the record... level with me, Jim."

Gordon stared at Chambers, then took a deep breath and let it out slowly. "You're right," he said. "I do know him. In a sense. I don't know who he really is, but I know *what* he is. We've met on a number of occasions. The first time was when he saved the life of my son. I owe him for that, Reese. And I owe him for lots more, besides. Look around you. This place is full of cops. Ask any one of them and they will tell you that as far as they're concerned, the Batman's one of *them*. Oh, they'd never say it for the record, they all know better, but it's how they really feel. And it's how *I* feel, too. But if you ever tell anyone I said that, I'll deny it. Unless you're wired and you've got it all on tape."

Chambers smiled. "You know better than that."

Gordon returned the smile. "Yes, I suppose I do, otherwise I never would have said what I said. We started off on the wrong foot, you and I, but you're a good man, Reese. And if this thing costs you your job with the Bureau, you can have a detective's gold shield in Gotham City anytime." He grimaced. "Assuming they don't toss *me* out on my keester."

"You think they will?"

Gordon shrugged. "It's always a possibility, but I rather doubt it. I make a convenient whipping boy. Besides, in this town, I know where all the bodies are buried."

Chambers grinned. "I'll bet you do. I checked you out, you know. I found out about what happened in Chicago. That took guts. And I found out about what happened here, as well. You took down the corrupt political machine and cleaned up this town virtually single-handed."

"Not single-handed," Gordon said. "Not by a long shot. I had help. Unofficial help."

"The Batman?"

"The Batman."

Chambers nodded. "I think I'm beginning to understand. He's sort of like your secret weapon, isn't he?"

"In a way," said Gordon. "But the Batman is no one's tool. If I ever became dirty, he'd take me down as well."

"Is he really that good?"

"He's really that good."

"I've been doing a lot of thinking about him lately," Chambers said. "The Bureau is aware of him, of course, but they don't take him very seriously. I think maybe that's a mistake. He's a lot more than just some kind of dramatic vigilante. I saw that chopper he took off in. It looked like something out of *Star Wars*. A real hi-tech, NOTAR design. Choppers like that are still in the prototype stage. It's not exactly something you can order up from a department store. If I didn't know better, I'd think the Batman was some kind of special government agent. Only, I can't think of any government agency that would run such an off-the-wall operation. That's like something out of a paperback novel. Although some of the things the Company does aren't that far off."

Gordon shook his head. "I considered that as well," he said. "But it simply doesn't add up. The CIA pulls off a lot of clandestine operations, some of them pretty outrageous, but how the hell could you keep someone like the Batman a secret? The network of support that would have to be involved, the complex logistics, his highly visible profile . . . Sooner or later, something somewhere would simply have to leak out. Too many people would know."

Chambers nodded again. "Yeah, I see your point. So the Batman's working on his own. But how the hell does he manage it? Where does he come up with his resources? You figure maybe he's got some gung-ho millionaire behind him? Someone like Ross Perot? What?"

Gordon smiled. "I gave up trying to figure it out," he said. "There was a time when I felt just the way you do now. I even had a list of likely suspects, but none of them panned out. I suppose if somebody who really knew what he was doing tried long enough and hard enough, he might be able to find out who the Batman is, but I'm not that somebody. I don't *want* to know. My knowing would make him vulnerable and lessen his effectiveness. And it would make *me* vulnerable as well, to the same kind of pressures you and I are facing now. What I don't know, I can't tell. That's not usually my attitude, but in this case, I think I'm better off."

Chambers pursed his lips thoughtfully. "What if I said I'd like to meet him? Just you and me, on whatever terms he wants. Could you set it up?"

Gordon stared at him for a long moment. "Maybe."

"Would you be willing to try?"

"If you're thinking of trying to take him, Reese, you may be biting off a lot more than you chew. No offense."

"None taken. I'll play it any way you like. You can have my piece and check me for a wire, anything you want. I'm not trying to pull a fast one. I just want to talk to the guy. Find out what makes him tick. After all, my career, for what's it worth, is sort of in his hands now."

Gordon nodded. "I'll see what I can do. But I'm not making any promises."

"Fair enough." He reached for the check.

"Let me get it," Gordon said.

"No, it's all right," Chambers said. "This time it's on the Bureau. What the hell, I may not have an expense account much longer."

"How's our guest doing?" Bruce asked Alfred, who wasn't looking very much like Alfred today. He had changed out of his habitual elegant, dark suit into a muted brown Harris tweed sport coat, a button-down white shirt with a silk ascot, gray flannel slacks, and cordovan wing tips. He wore a wig of dark brown hair liberally streaked with gray, and he had added a matching full beard that covered his neatly trimmed greying moustache. He had completed the makeup job with a pair of horn-rimmed glasses, and he was completely unrecognizable. He could have chosen any of a number of disguises, but he had chosen to look like an avuncular college professor, nonthreatening yet still with associations of subtle control. It was a choice that said much about Alfred's perceptions.

The butler sighed. "She can be a rather trying young person, Master Bruce."

"Trying? In what way?"

"She is very confused, and highly irritable, and her method of attempting to exercise some level of control over her environment is to present a rather challenging, abrasive, and altogether unpleasant exterior. It seems to be her way of keeping people at a distance, of attempting to appear confident and self-assured, but inside she is a very frightened young woman."

"I know, Alfred," Bruce said. "Try to be patient with her. She hasn't had an easy life."

"I gathered that," Alfred replied. "She seemed to become especially disturbed after she saw the evening news tonight."

"I don't blame her," Bruce said. "That was a very disturbing newscast."

He sighed heavily. The late news had reported Specter's answer to his taped remarks. They had also reported the tragic statistics of the bombing. Over two hundred and fifty dead. Close to a hundred critically injured. And as yet, an undetermined number still to be found beneath the wreckage. He felt almost completely numb. The only emotion he was capable of feeling at the moment was cold rage, and it took all his considerable willpower to keep that rage under control. He would need that rage, he would use it, but it *had* to be controlled, for the alternative was too frightening to contemplate.

"I may have made a bad mistake in baiting him," he said. "It looks as though his acts of terror toward the city will continue. He's not playing into my hands as planned."

"If you are referring to his threat to commit additional terrorist acts especially to spite you, Master Bruce," said Alfred, "then you risk falling into the trap that he has set for you."

Bruce frowned. "How's that, Alfred?"

"I know something of the terrorist mind," Alfred replied, "from my days with the Special Air Service. The terrorist seeks to manipulate. He seeks to control, through fear and guilt and uncertainty. If Specter is able to convince you that you bear part of the responsibility for his actions, then he has already won half the battle, Master Bruce. You did not create him. You are not responsible for him or for anything he does. He has a mission, a contract, that he has undertaken of his own free will, and I expect he has been very well paid for it. You had no part in that. Even had you remained completely uninvolved, it would not have changed a thing."

"Perhaps," said Bruce, "but I'm afraid the people will blame me for inciting him to even greater levels of violence."

"Possibly," Alfred replied, "and without a doubt, some people *will* blame you, those who already disapprove of what you're doing. But I think you may be underestimating the citizens of Gotham City. They know what you stand for. And, conversely, they know what Specter stands for as well."

"I hope you're right, Alfred," Bruce said. "But I can't remember when I felt so powerless. Perhaps not since the day my parents were killed. Specter has succeeded in eluding some of the finest intelligence and law-enforcement agencies in the entire world. How do I find such a man in a city of over two million people?"

"I'm afraid I do not possess the answer to that question, Master Bruce," said Alfred. "It is why the terrorist is the most loathsome and dangerous of creatures. He strikes always from the shadows, indiscriminately, and he remains faceless and unknown. If he is betrayed by someone in his own organization, or if you can succeed in infiltrating that organization, then he may be defeated. Otherwise, the only way to stop him is if he makes some sort of mistake or if you can somehow anticipate his actions."

"Specter doesn't strike me as a man who makes mistakes," said Bruce. "His long record of successful assassinations testifies to that. And when it comes to anticipating his actions, how can I possibly do that? His targets of opportunity in Gotham City are virtually limitless. And I am just one man."

"Correction, Master Bruce," said Alfred. "You are not just one man. You have friends among the people of this city. Those who, like Commissioner Gordon, owe you a debt of gratitude. It strikes me that now may be the time to collect upon that debt."

He had taught his last class of the day several hours ago and had just finished his meditations when he sensed a familiar presence in the dojo.

"You are early tonight, Masked Rodent," he called out from behind the screen separating his private quarters from the remainder of the loft.

"Sensei, I need your help," the Batman said.

Sato came out from behind the partition, barefoot and dressed in a long, flowing, black silk robe. "It is the one who calls himself Specter, is it not?"

"Yes."

Sato nodded. "Come. Sit. I have just made some tea for myself."

They sat in their accustomed corner on cushions placed around the low, black lacquered table.

"I had wondered when you would come to ask about this man," said Sato, pouring them some tea.

"I did not wish to inflict my problems on others," said the Batman.

"A man like this is everybody's problem," the old man replied. "He has declared war upon the people of this city, a war that he prosecutes by dishonorable means. Such a man cannot be tolerated."

"There is almost nothing known about him," said the Batman. "I need to find him, so that I can stop him, but I don't even know where to begin. I've never encountered an enemy like this. There is no pattern to his actions. No way to anticipate where he will strike next. I feel completely powerless against him. I—"

Sato cut him off with an abrupt chopping motion of his hand. "No man is powerless who has the ability to think," he said. "You must divorce yourself from your emotions. Think with this," he said, tapping a finger to his forehead, "and not with this." He put his hand against his heart.

"It's difficult not to feel the pain he's caused," the Batman said.

Sato nodded. "Yes. That is his greatest weapon. You feel the pain that he has brought into the world. You feel outrage, and you feel anger, and these emotions make you feel powerless. When two opponents face each other in combat, the one who is the first to anger is the one who has already lost."

"How is it possible *not* to feel the anger?"

"It is not possible," the old man replied.

"Sensei, please," the Batman said. "I don't need your riddles tonight."

"No riddle," Sato said. There is anger that can fuel one's actions and control one's responses, and there is anger that is a function of awareness. It is the latter type of which you and I must speak. The anger that controls is the anger that prevents one from thinking clearly. The anger that is a level of awareness can be a powerful, motivating force, the energies of which can be effectively channeled, but only if one controls that energy, rather than allowing it to control him. It requires discipline, discipline that you possess in abundance. However, in your anger you have allowed yourself to become undisciplined. The force rages within you, with no direction and no outlet, and it makes you feel powerless. You have lost the battle before you have even begun."

"How can I win?" the Batman asked.

"Do not seek to sublimate your rage," the old man said. "Seek, rather, to contain it as a part of your awareness. It will serve to remind you why you do what you must do. Your enemy expects you to feel rage. He knows that it will force you to make mistakes or render you powerless to act. In your awareness of your anger at your enemy, know that the emotion is a tool that either one of you may use. Do not give him the satisfaction of using it against you. Temper your rage with calm deliberation. Know your enemy, and know the tools and weapons that he uses. To defeat him, you must learn to think as he does. You must become as one with him."

"Do you mean that to defeat Specter, I must become exactly like him?" asked the Batman. "That's something I've fought against all my life."

"No," said Sato, shaking his head. "You must not be exactly *like* your enemy, you must *become* your enemy. You must make yourself think the way he does. Anticipate how he may respond. Consider how *you* would proceed if you were in his place."

"Think like a terrorist, like an assassin," said the Batman.

"Exactly. This is a man who feels no remorse, no empathy for his victims. What he does, he does not out of passion, but out of cold deliberation. He considers the lives he takes merely as a means to a desired end. He has removed emotion from his consideration. If, in sending him your challenge, you succeed in arousing emotion within him, then you will succeed in altering the conditions under which he functions best."

"So you don't think it was a mistake?" the Batman asked.

"I have seen the news tonight," Sato replied. "It was reported that Specter telephoned the station and replied to your challenge. It was not necessary for him to do so."

"But I took his target," the Batman replied. "I have something he wants."

"Do you? As I understand the situation, his primary goal is to pressure the authorities to release General Garcia. To foment fear and panic in the city in order to bring that pressure to bear. He does not have to deal with you to do this. If his secondary goal is to eliminate this witness, both to prevent damaging testimony and as an object lesson to others who might be tempted to turn on his employers, then would it not be just as simple for him to strike when the witness appears before the court? It is the one time when he can be certain where that individual will be. And if he has doubts as to that witness's identity, could he not place a bomb somewhere within the courthouse building? He has already demonstrated his callous disregard for human life. What difference does it make to him if others die at the same time?"

"Well, to play devil's advocate," the Batman said, "the courthouse will be heavily guarded, for one thing. Everyone going in and out will be carefully searched, and anything that they bring in will be passed through detectors."

"That has not stopped clever men before," Sato pointed out.

"No, maybe not," the Batman conceded. "But if he bombs the courthouse, he also risks killing Garcia."

"Perhaps that makes no difference to him," Sato said. "Perhaps, if he cannot succeed in effecting General Garcia's release, killing him would be the only remaining option."

"It's possible," the Batman said.

"If I were an assassin," Sato said, "and you had hidden the one I wished to kill from me, and I had no more regard for human life than Specter has, I would take a hostage and demand that you gave up my quarry to me in return for the life of that hostage. If you did not comply, I would kill my hostage, in a manner that would bring about a great deal of horror and revulsion, and I would then take another hostage. Perhaps two. If you again refused to comply with my demands, next time I would increase the number and continue in the same vein, until I forced you to my will. One life for the lives of many. Is that not the equation that governs Specter's actions in the case of General Garcia?"

"Yes, that's exactly what I'm afraid he's going to do," the Batman said. "He's already promised to blow up not one, but two targets next, one exclusively for my benefit."

"Then we understand the way he thinks," said Sato, "and that is not your responsibility. That is a choice that *he* has made. I suspect he would have done so regardless of whether the witness was in your custody or the hands of the police. You have not condemned anyone to death by what you have done, my friend. Rather, you have saved one life. The life of the witness. You must now attempt to save others. You may not succeed. But there is honor in making the attempt. Remember one thing. The main difference between you and this assassin is that to you, the thought of killing is abhorrent. So long as you continue to protect the witness, you are engaged in saving life. *He* is the one committing murder, not you. However, if you give in to his demands, to his attempts to manipulate your emotions, and release the witness to his mercy, then you will no longer be engaged in saving life, but in participating in a killing. It is a cold logic, but it is what must support you in what you choose to do. Do you accept this?"

The Batman nodded. "Yes, Sensei. I accept it."

"Good. Then we shall now begin to think like assassins, you and I. I have some more experience in this, and I will attempt to guide you. We already know his goals, and we already know that there *is* a pattern to his actions. You were wrong in saying there was no such pattern. It is self-evident. He will seek to horrify the people of this city by striking at targets that will ensure spectacular results—that is to say, many deaths at once, brought about in such a manner as to excite a great deal of emotion. Let us think as he does, and select targets of our own, as many as we can think of. Then we will attempt to place eyes and ears around those targets."

"There aren't enough cops in this city to watch every possible target," said the Batman.

"We shall look not only to the police for our assistance, but also to those whom this assassin has chosen for his enemies. The people of this city. One hunter, stalking his prey alone, will not be as successful as the one who has others to beat the bushes and drive the prey to him."

"A . . . a friend of mine said almost exactly the same thing," said the Batman.

"Then your friend is wise, and you would do well to heed his counsel. I have many students. And they each have many friends. And their friends will have friends. That is a beginning. Have you no friends to whom you may turn?"

The Batman nodded. "Yes. I think I may have a few."

"A man with a few friends is wealthy beyond measure," Sato said. "Together, let us tap our wealth, and we shall buy defeat for Specter. Now, let us consider where we would place our bombs if we wanted to murder many people at one time . . ."

He had ordered a limousine to pick him up at the Gotham Plaza Hotel. He said he would pay cash to the driver and gave his name as "Mr. Devon Stuart, of Bloodstar Records." He said he would be having a conference in the hotel bar and asked to be called there when the car arrived.

When the driver saw him coming out of the hotel, he saw a man with below-the-shoulder-length black hair, designer sunglasses, an expensive black leather jacket worn over a white silk shirt, a matching white silk scarf draped around his neck, tight black leather trousers with a silver concha belt, and high-heeled boots, one of which had a gold chain wrapped around it. He was also carrying an attaché case.

"Mr. Stuart" got into the back seat and gave his destination as Club 34, *the* hot spot in Gotham City, where the beautiful people went to dance and meet each other, to see and to be seen. The door attendants at the club, whose job it was to decide which of the people lined up outside would be allowed in—choices often influenced by physical appearance alone, or by fashion sense, or a folded twenty-dollar bill discreetly slipped and palmed—saw the long white limousine pull up, saw the chauffeur open the door for someone who had "rock star" or "record producer" written all over him, and deduced that he had to be someone important and quickly ushered him inside.

Once inside the club, Specter paused briefly to take in the atmosphere: the earthshakingly loud rock music blaring from concert-hall speakers; the colored, flashing lights; the mixed odors of body sweat, perfume, and cologne; the gyrating couples on the dance floor and those seeking to impress each other at the bar; the ones who had succeeded in impressing each other fondling and kissing at the tables and in dark corners. Expensive clothes, expensive drinks, cheap thrills. He made his way over to the bar and attracted the attention of the bartender by holding up a fifty-dollar bill.

"Yes, sir, what can I get for you tonight?"

"Just a glass of water, thanks, but this is yours if

you'd be so kind as to take care of this case for me. I wouldn't want to risk losing it in the crowd, and I'm hesitant to check it."

"Sure thing, sir, no problem. I'll just keep it here behind the bar, where I can keep an eye on it."

"Thanks ever so much."

"No problem. Jeez, this thing's heavy. What've you got in here?"

"It's filled with high explosives."

"Yeah, right." The bartender grinned. "I'll handle it real careful."

"Thank you. I appreciate that."

"My pleasure, sir." He pocketed the fifty.

Specter lit up one of his French cigarettes and sipped his water.

"Hi."

He turned to see a young woman with long, honey-blond hair, pouting lips, a pretty face, and an extremely close-fitting and short dress with a plunging neckline that left very little to the imagination.

"Hello."

"My name's Linda. What's yours?"

"Devon."

"Devon. What a lovely name. You sound English."

He smiled.

"I haven't seen you around here before. What do you do?"

"I'm a professional assassin."

She giggled. "Have you assassinated many people?"

"Oh, sure, lots. What do you do?"

"That depends on what you like. Want to dance?"

They moved out onto the dance floor. She danced close

152 / SIMON HAWKE

to him, making lots of eye and body contact, and after a few moments, they came into one another's arms and she tilted her head back so that he could kiss her.

"Mmm," she moaned into his ear, "you're a great kisser. I could get a real bang out of you."

"Yes, I'm sure you will. Excuse me a moment, will you? I've got to find the little boy's room. Be a good little girl and wait for me by the bar?"

"Sure, babe. Hurry back."

He threaded his way through the crowd and slipped out through the fire door. He tossed the wig and glasses into a Dumpster, went down the alley to the sidewalk, and strolled calmly to the corner. Once he reached the corner, he paused by a public phone booth and glanced at his watch.

"Good-bye, Linda," he said.

The explosion was powerful enough to rip through the entire front of the building, killing most of the people lined up on the sidewalk outside. At the same time, another bomb, in a similar attaché case, went off in the Gotham Plaza Hotel. Specter picked up the phone and dialed a number. A recording answered.

"Hi, this is Enrique. I'm not home right now, but if you'll leave your name and number and a brief message at the sound of the tone, I'll get back to you as soon as I can." The machine beeped.

"This is Specter. Yes, I know where you live. However, there's no need to be nervous. We're old friends, you and I. I thought you might care to know that I've just detonated a bomb at the Gotham Plaza Hotel. That was to remind everyone about General Garcia. I've also just blown up Club 34. That was for the Batman's interference in my affairs. Do give him my warmest regards, will you? Have a nice day."

He hung up the phone and went off, whistling, down the street.

"Hi, this is Paul Santone..."

"...and I'm Jody Dennis, and welcome to *Good Morning, Gotham*."

"Normally at this point," Santone said, "we tell you what our lineup of guests is going to be, and then we sit and chat a bit before we go to Bill Johansen for the morning news and weather, but in light of the terrible events of last night, we find it difficult, it not impossible, to be our usual cheerful selves this morning. For the benefit of those of you who don't yet know about the double tragedy that struck this city during the night, we're going to go straight to Bill Johansen in the newsroom. Bill?"

The camera cut to a middle-aged man in a gray suit and a red tie sitting behind a desk in the newsroom.

"Yes, terrible events indeed, Paul. Last night, at approximately one A.M., Specter struck again. Not once, but twice, and with tragic and devastating consequences. Gotham was still reeling from the bombing of Barrington's department store when Specter once again made good his threat to bring terror to the people of this city. At approximately the same time, bombs were detonated at the Gotham Plaza Hotel and the chic Club 34 nightclub. At this hour, fire fighters, after working throughout the night, have managed to bring the flames under control at the Club 34 location, but the Gotham Plaza Hotel is still burning as we speak. For a live update, we go now to Ron Mathews at the Gotham Plaza. Can you hear me, Ron?"

The camera cut to a shot of a young reporter in a trenchcoat standing across the street from the flaming hotel. In the background, a number of fire trucks were visible, with fire fighters manning hoses. The still-dark, early-morning sky was lit up with the flashing lights of police squad cars and ambulances. A small graphic at the bottom of the screen gave the station logo and read, "Live."

"Yes, I can hear you, Bill," Ron Mathews said, pressing his earpiece close, "but it's difficult with all this noise out here. I've been hearing sirens ever since I got here. That and the screams of the people trapped inside that horrible inferno. This is a site of chaos and utter mayhem as I stand here on the far side of the plaza, which is as close as the police will allow anyone to come. Despite the early hour, the sidewalks in front of me, beyond the barricades, are thronged with people, all staring in shock and disbelief at the carnage that has taken place here.

"No one seems to know exactly how it happened, and I don't know if you can see it from here, but from where I stand, I see that the entire left front section of the Gotham Plaza Hotel—that would be your left and my right—is just completely gone, as if it were struck by a guided missile. Part of the building has collapsed, and the rest is all in flames. By the time fire fighters arrived upon the scene, the flames were completely out of control, raging throughout the entire building. It's been a long, hard night for the Gotham City Fire Department, and for the police as well. Here with me is Gotham City fire fighter Dan Zambrowski, who has, in spite of his obvious exhaustion, consented to speak with us briefly while he is taking a very much-needed break...."

The shot widened as a weary fire fighter stepped into the frame.

"Dan, I know you must be tired, and a few moments ago, I saw you taking oxygen.... This must have been a dreadful night for you. How are the fire fighters holding up?"

"About as well as could be expected, Ron. I gotta get back in there in a few minutes, after I've caught my breath... Jesus, it's just hell in there. At this point, we're just doing everything we can to get the people out. We know there's still a lot of people trapped on the upper floors... we've been using helicopters to take some people off the roof who've made it up there, but... it's still not all of them, not by a long shot...."

"Do you have any idea what sort of bomb it was?"

"Man, I don't know... I'm not an expert. We figure it hadda to be set off somewhere on the first floor, but whatever it was, it was one hell of an incendiary device. It blew out the whole front of the building, and the place went up like someone napalmed it."

"How long do you think it will take before you get the fire under control?"

"I don't know... we're hoping maybe in the next hour or so. But it's hard to tell... Our first priority is trying to get those people out."

"The damage to the building looks very extensive."

"Man, it's a total loss. I mean, I don't know... I

could be wrong, I guess, but I don't see any way it's not gonna have to be demolished."

"Do you have any idea of the death toll?"

The fire fighter shook his head. "Oh, God, don't ask me that. I don't even want to think about it. I've been a fire fighter for fifteen years, and this has been the worst night of my life. Look, I gotta go...."

"Of course, I understand. Thank you for the taking the time to talk with us. Be careful out there, Dan."

"Yeah. Thanks."

"Well, you heard him. He said he's been a fire fighter for fifteen years and this has been the worst night of his life. I guess that says it all. Back to you, Bill."

"Thank you, Ron. You'll be standing by to keep us posted."

"Yes, I will."

"And as if that sight wasn't grim enough, we go now to Susan Shapiro at Club 34. Susan?"

The shot showed a good-looking, young brunette in a black leather coat standing across the street from the wreckage that was the Club 34 nightclub.

"Bill, behind me is what's left of the chic Gotham City night spot once known as Club 34. I really don't know how to begin trying to describe this scene to you.... We'll just train our camera across the street and you can see it for yourself."

"My God," said Bill Johansen, off camera.

"Words simply fail me," said Susan Shapiro. "Only a short while ago, fire fighters finally got the flames put out and, as you can clearly see, what's left is nothing but a smoking ruin. It resembles a war zone out here. This could be Beirut, or Dresden after the firebombing of

World War II. I've never seen anything like it. At this point, police and fire fighters are combing through the smoking wreckage, searching for bodies and any possible survivors, though it's hard to believe that anyone could have survived in there. It's . . . it's just unbelievable."

"Susan," Johansen interrupted, "is there any way of knowing how many people were inside?"

"Bill, it's impossible to speculate. The club was packed. It was a Saturday night, always their busiest night of the week, and many people were turned away at the doors. I have an actual eyewitness to the explosion here with me. Sir, would you step over here, please?"

A young man in sharp, fashionable clothes stepped into the frame, but his leather jacket was covered with dust and his white shirt, open at the neck, was filthy. His hair was in a state of disarray.

"Your name is . . ."

"Romanelli. Tony Romanelli."

"Mr. Romanelli, to explain your appearance, we should point out that you've been here all night, assisting in the rescue efforts."

"Yeah, that's right. I mean, I couldn't just leave, you know? Christ, I had to *do* something."

"Is it true that you were actually on line outside the club shortly before the bomb went off?"

"Yeah, that's right. I ran outta cigarettes and I asked the guy behind me to save my place while I ran to the bar across the street to get some more."

"And that's what saved your life?"

"Yeah. Can you believe it? And I was going to quit smoking. Just about everybody on that line was killed. Jeez, it's unbelievable. I'm *still* shakin'."

"So you were in the bar across the street when the bomb went off?"

"Yeah. I'd just walked in to use the cigarette machine. The thing went off not five seconds after I got inside. It's a walk-down, so there's like only a small window by the door, and it got blown out. You could actually *feel* it in there. The mirror behind the bar broke, the bottles broke, some of the people sitting by the door got knocked right off their seats."

"Clear across the street?"

"Yeah, that's right."

"Was there anyone with you on that line? I mean, had you come to the club alone?"

"I was with a couple of my friends from work. I don't know what happened to them. I figure they're gone. I mean, it's strange, you know, it still hasn't really hit me. I'm just feelin' sort of numb. I can't go home. I mean, if I do, I know I'm gonna fall apart. I just can't deal with that right now. I don't want to talk about it anymore, okay?"

"Of course. Thank you, Mr. Romanelli. You're a very lucky man."

"Yeah, I guess I am. Funny thing. I don't feel very lucky right now."

"Back to you, Bill."

"Thank you, Susan. We have Ross Carter standing by at Gotham General Hospital..."

Alfred walked over to the television set and turned it off without a word.

"Leave it on," said Bruce.

"No, Master Bruce," said Alfred gently. "You've

seen quite enough. Don't do this to yourself. You've been up all night. You need some rest."

Bruce Wayne looked up at him with a stricken expression. "How, Alfred?" he said hoarsely. "*How* can I rest with a monster like that out there, who can strike again at any time? *How?* You tell me!"

"You will need your strength," said Alfred. "You will need full use of your faculties, perhaps as you never did before. I know it will be difficult to sleep. I can administer a mild sedative...."

"I'll only dream about it, Alfred. The reality is grotesque enough. I can't face the nightmares."

"You must rest, Master Bruce. You *must*."

"There will be no rest for me, Alfred. Not so long as *he* is out there." He got up from his chair. "I'm going to the Batcave. I have work to do."

CHAPTER
EIGHT

"I didn't think you'd be able to set it up so fast," said Chambers as they drove across the bridge in Gordon's car.

"I didn't," Gordon replied. "The Batman asked for this meeting. And he specifically requested to see you."

"No kidding? How'd he get in touch?"

"By telephone," said Gordon. "And if you're thinking of asking about a trace, forget it. It's been tried."

"And?"

"We wound up chasing our own tails all over the city. Somehow, he's able to tie into the phone-company computer lines and drop little gremlins into the system. Gotham Bell just about had a hemorrhage trying to figure out exactly what he did and how he did it. They never did find out."

"So he's a computer hacker on top of everything else?"

"The Batman is a lot of things," said Gordon.

"You know, I hate to admit it, but I'm starting to have a sort of sneaking admiration for the guy. Go figure it."

"It isn't hard to figure at all," said Gordon. "I'm a cop. You're a G-man. Either one of us could have made a lot more money doing something else, only we didn't. Why? Maybe because our fathers were both in law enforcement. Maybe because Matt Dillon made a big impression on us when we were kids, or maybe it was Tom Mix or Red Ryder or the Duke."

Chambers grinned. "Not my generation," he said. "For me, it was Bob Conrad in *Wild, Wild West*."

"Government agent, always wore a suit, never cracked a smile," Gordon said. "Yep. Figures you'd join the FBI."

Chambers chuckled. "You really think it's as simple as all that?"

"Of course not," said Gordon, "but it's an important factor. Our values are shaped by the heroes we had as children. Maybe it isn't something we consciously think about anymore, but it's there."

"Who was it for you?" asked Chambers.

"Don't laugh."

"Okay, I promise."

"The Green Hornet."

"The Green Hornet?"

"You promised not to laugh."

"I'm not laughing. But... the *Green Hornet*? Why an old radio show hero?"

"I suppose because to me, as a child, the Green Hornet represented goodness. He was pure. There weren't any gray areas for him. A man was either good or he was bad. And if he was good, there weren't certain situations in which it was okay to be bad, or even a little bit bad. There was no compromise."

"No situational ethics," Chambers said.

"Right. Though as a kid, what did I know about situational ethics? All I knew was that if you were good, you *did* good. You helped other people. And the closest thing I had to the Green Hornet was my old man."

"Who was a cop."

"Just an ordinary beat cop in Chicago," Gordon said. "And at a time when a lot of cops in Chicago were corrupt. But not my dad. Everybody in the neighborhood knew what my father stood for. Men took their hats off to him when we walked down the street. He cared about people and he tried to help them. He was a big man, and he was strong, and he was good, and it didn't seem as if there was anything he couldn't do. To me, my dad was just like the Green Hornet."

"So you became a cop," said Chambers, nodding. "Yeah, it makes perfect sense." He sighed. "But it's different being a cop these days. You ever regret your choice?"

"Not for a second."

"Really?"

"Really. Why, do you?"

"Sometimes," Chambers admitted. "There was a time when you had to be a lawyer to join the Bureau. That's changed, of course, but sometimes I wonder if I wouldn't have been better off as a lawyer."

"As a prosecutor, of course," said Gordon.

"Of course. So I could get the bad guys. Or maybe a writer."

"A *writer*?"

"Yeah. Then I'd write stories that always had happy endings. Stories where the good guys always win. Stories where innocent people don't get hurt and the world is a better place to live in."

"You'd go broke," said Gordon.

"Yeah, you're probably right."

They pulled off into a picnic area set well back from the road in a grove of trees.

"This the place?" said Chambers.

"No, we're going to have a picnic," Gordon said.

"Very funny."

They got out of the car.

Chambers looked around. "It's isolated, but it doesn't seem like the most secure area in the world. Isn't he worried about a trap?"

"No, he isn't," said a deep voice from the shadows.

Chambers's hand instinctively went for his gun, but Gordon had relieved him of it earlier. He had insisted, and it was locked in the trunk of the car.

The Batman stepped out from the shadows. Chambers had been prepared for the unique costume, but not for the appearance of the man himself. He stood over six feet tall, and he was built like Mr. Olympia. That wasn't padding underneath that suit, it was solid muscle. And there was something else, as well. The man had an incredible presence. It wasn't only the way he looked, but the way he held himself, the way he moved...He *commanded* attention. Chambers slowly took his hand out from inside his jacket, where there was only an empty holster.

"Hello, Commissioner. And you must be Mr. Chambers."

He stepped forward and offered Chambers his hand. The grip was strong.

"Aren't you taking a big chance meeting me?" asked Chambers. "What if I'd had a gun and pulled it on you?"

"I would have taken it away from you," the Batman said, and the way he said it, so calmly and matter-of-factly, Chambers was left with no doubt that he could easily have done it. "Besides," the Batman continued, "it isn't really me you want. It's Specter."

"You can say that again," said Chambers. "Right now, you're the least of my concerns. You know what the bastard did last night?"

"Yes," the Batman said softly. "I know. That's why I asked to meet with you. He *must* be stopped."

"We're in agreement there," said Chambers. "By the way, how's my witness?"

"Miss Morrison is well and comfortable. You need have no concern on her account, I assure you. She will be present in court to testify against Garcia."

"You're not finding her a bit of a handful?" Chambers asked.

"She's had a difficult life," the Batman said. "One must try to make allowances."

"Tell me something," Chambers said. "How did you manage to pull it off?"

"I have my methods," said the Batman. He turned to Gordon. "I'm sorry about the necessity of knocking out your men, Commissioner, but I didn't want to risk injuring anyone. Please convey my apologies to them."

"I'll do that," Gordon said.

"Mr. Chambers, I owe you my apologies as well. It was not my intention to interfere with you or with the Commissioner, but I was very much concerned about the safety of all the parties involved. I was afraid that Specter might seek to intimidate the Commissioner by threatening his family. I am immune to such threats, as I am immune to political pressure and to the possibility of any leaks."

"I appreciate the sentiment," said Chambers, "but you realize this makes you guilty of kidnapping, and a host of other offenses? By rights, I ought to be arresting you."

"I understand that," said the Batman. "However, I think we can all agree that this is an extraordinary situation, if we succeed, then I suspect it won't be difficult to get the kidnapping charge dropped. As for any other charges, well, I suppose I'll have to live with them."

"Just tell me one thing," Chambers said. "You're obviously a highly intelligent and resourceful man. Someone who could do anything he wanted with his life. Why choose this?"

"What makes you think I had a choice?" the Batman replied. "Why do you do what you do?"

"That's different," Chambers said. "I work within the system. You could have chosen to do that as well."

The Batman shook his head. "I wouldn't have been nearly as effective. The system has certain limitations, as I'm sure you know. Criminals are not afraid of the system. They've learned how to manipulate it. They are afraid of me precisely because they know that I am not restrained by the system."

"But it's well known that you don't kill," said Chambers. "Or at least you try not to."

"No, I do not kill," the Batman said. "The thought of murder is abhorrent to me. But I can punish them. I can humiliate them in the eyes of their peers. I can make them afraid. And that is something the police cannot do. However, I didn't ask you here in order to justify myself or to explain my methods. We must stop Specter, and time is precious."

"Okay," said Chambers, "I'm listening."

"The task force you've assembled is insufficient to the job at hand," the Batman said. "We must attempt to anticipate Specter's actions. It's the only way he will be stopped. Unless I can bait him into coming after me directly, which is what I hope to do, by infuriating him."

"What've you got on your mind?"

"I have assembled a sort of task force of my own," the Batman said, "composed of citizens of Gotham City."

"Now, wait a minute—" Chambers began, but the Batman held up his hand and he fell silent.

"Hear me out. These people have been given strict instructions to avoid direct involvement. Their primary task is one of surveillance."

"Who are these people?" Gordon asked.

"Some of them are familiar to you, Commissioner. The Green Dragons, for example."

"The Green Dragons?" Chambers said. "What is that, a street gang?"

"Not exactly," Gordon replied. "The Green Dragons are a group of young people, primarily of Asian extraction, who act as a sort of neighborhood protective association in Chinatown. They range in age from eighteen, which is the minimum age you can be to join, to late twenties, although a few of the members of their council are in their thirties. They are all highly trained martial artists, they don't carry any weapons, and they essentially patrol the streets at night and assist in various community projects during the day.''

"Like the Guardian Angels in New York?" asked Chambers.

"Essentially similar," said the Batman. "They have agreed to volunteer their services, as have the Gotham City cabbies, among others who have unanimously voted to give up some of their off-duty hours to the task."

"What task is that?" asked Chambers.

"The task of attempting to anticipate Specter," said the Batman. "Based on what I know of him and what I've been able to deduce, I have compiled a list of possible targets where he may strike. Here is a copy of that list." He handed a computer printout to Chambers. "Those marked with an asterisk are the most likely targets. Each of these locations will have observers assigned to it. I have arranged for them all to be equipped with two-way radios that will enable them to keep in touch with your task force. To avoid confusion, they will not be using the standard police frequency. The frequency they'll be using is marked on the printout."

"How the hell will they know if Specter shows up at any of these locations?" Chambers asked. "These are all areas with a lot of public traffic going in and out. He could be anybody."

"Not just anybody," said the Batman. "We know that he's a male, probably European, and we know that the nature of the explosive he uses, and the amount needed to achieve his desired results, renders the device too large for him to carry comfortably on his person. He could have the disassembled components distributed about his body, and then try to assemble the device at the site of his chosen target, but that would be too time-consuming and too risky. Instead, he will probably carry the device in an attaché case, or perhaps a shoulder bag, either one of which would look most natural and would not attract any attention. The citizen observer teams will all receive special briefing printouts, instructing them what to look for and how to act. If they spot anything suspicious, they will radio in to police headquarters at once."

"Great. So we're looking for a man with a shoulder bag or a briefcase. You have any idea how many false leads we're liable to wind up chasing?" Chambers said.

"It's better than no leads at all," the Batman replied. "But there is more that we can do. When Specter entered the country, he had to have gone through customs. Entering the country illegally would have entailed added risk, and would have involved parties he probably couldn't afford to trust. So he either entered the country on a tourist or a business visa, or he came in under diplomatic credentials. Whether they were forged or genuine is immaterial. The point is, there will be a record of his entry."

"You have any idea how long it will take to sort through all of those?" said Chambers. "Even if we start from the date of Garcia's arrival in the city, it could take weeks."

"Perhaps for you, but not for me," the Batman said, "I have equipment that will greatly help speed up the task. In fact, I am already on it. Nor is that all. Specter has to have a base of operations somewhere in this city. He wouldn't choose any of the embassies, since he might easily be spotted that way by surveillance. Nor would he choose a hotel, since he could be tracked there as well."

"I know," said Chambers. "We've been checking into that."

"That leaves only two other likely possibilities," said Batman. "I considered the fact that he might be staying at a location rented for him by his employers, but again the risk of being traced that way would be too great, and it wouldn't fit his *modus operandi*. Specter is a very careful man. So that means he's either found someone to stay with or he's subletting. I'd bet on the latter. It would be considerably less involved and would entail less risk. I'm already engaged in checking through all the ads in Gotham's newspapers that appeared in the time period we're dealing with, and I'm comparing that to telephone-company records."

"Phone-company records," Gordon said. "Of course! If he's subletting, then chances are whoever he's subletting from discontinued their service and he had the service reestablished."

"No, quite the opposite," the Batman said. "The technology exists to trace telephone calls almost instantaneously. Mr. Chambers will confirm that."

"Yes, he's right," said Chambers.

"And the situation you've described, Commissioner, would cover most situations with subletters," said the Batman. "However, what we're looking for is someone who sublet an apartment where the phone service had been discontinued by the original tenant, and then was *not* reestablished by the new tenant. Specter would use only public phones, and never the same one twice. And he would have wanted telephone service discontinued at his base of operations, for fear of an infinity transmitter."

"An infinity transmitter?" Gordon asked. "What's that?"

"A way of using a telephone as a surveillance device," said Chambers. "You can hang up, but the phone still remains live, and it can monitor everything in its location. But suppose Specter *did* reestablish phone service, and then merely disconnected the phone?"

"That's possible," the Batman said, "but I'm betting that he didn't do that. Establishing a new account with Gotham Bell can be complicated enough. I don't think he would have bothered with it."

"It all makes sense," said Chambers. "Still, it's a hell of a long shot."

"Perhaps," the Batman said, "but it's the most logical and methodical approach available to us. I can handle that end of it. Your job will be to coordinate with the citizen observers, chase down every possible lead you get, because you can't afford to ignore any of them, and have as many bomb-disposal experts standing by as you can get your hands on."

"I've already got that in the works," said Chambers. "We've got the Gotham City PD bomb squad, plus some of our own Bureau people and several teams the Army's sending in."

"Good," said the Batman. "And the final thing, Commissioner, is to put as much police presence on the streets as possible, particularly around those locations I've given you. Our immediate concern at this point is to make Specter's job as difficult as possible. Prevention first, then apprehension."

"It'll be done," said Gordon. "I'll cancel all leaves and put every available officer on the streets."

"What about the political situation?" asked the Batman. "Is there any chance you'll be forced to knuckle under to Specter's demands and release General Garcia?"

"Over my dead body," Chambers said.

"Realistically," said the Batman.

"Realistically, huh?" said Chambers sourly. "Yeah, I suppose there's a chance. Especially after what happened last night." He rubbed his forehead wearily. It was clear he hadn't been getting much rest at all. "Both Jim and I are getting it from all sides."

"The mayor's office is up in arms," said Gordon. "So is the city council. And the newspapers. I've also heard from the governor. I expect it will get worse."

"Right now, there's a lot of pressure to move Garcia to another city," said Chambers, "but who in their right mind would take him after this? Garcia is a federal prisoner, but if enough public pressure's brought to bear, and it's getting pretty bad, there's a good chance they'll wind up putting him on that plane to Cuba."

"That's what I was afraid of," said the Batman. "There is an alternative, you know."

"Don't even think it," Chambers said. "There's no way we can turn Garcia over to you. Not even if we make it look like an abduction, which is exactly what I suspect happened with our witness," he added, giving Gordon a wry look. "My job's hanging by a thread as it is, and it isn't just my job, believe me. If that's all it was, I might be tempted. But if you got your hands on him, the media and his goddamn lawyers would go absolutely berserk. No, Garcia's going to stay in maximums security and that's all there is to it."

"In that case, we haven't got much time," the Batman said. "I suggest we all get moving. Good talking with you, Mr. Chambers. Thank you for coming. Commissioner..."

He turned and melted into shadows, back into the trees.

"Where the hell do you suppose he's going?" Chambers asked, and a minute later his question was answered when a high-pitched, peculiar sound filled the air and they saw a Whirlybat ascending, a small, collapsible, one-man helicopter that consisted of little more than a seat, a prop, and an engine strapped to the pilot.

"I'll be damned," said Chambers. "Will you look at that? That guy's got more hi-tech gadgets than a James Bond movie!"

"Just be grateful that he's on our side," said Gordon.

"I hear you," Chambers said. He shook his head with amazement. "I think I finally understand the way you feel about him. He's really..." His voice trailed off as he searched for a way to put his thoughts into words.

"Something special?" Gordon offered.

"Yeah," said Chambers, nodding. "He's really something special. Only, do me a favor, okay? Don't go telling anyone about this. Somehow I don't think my superiors would understand."

"You think mine would?" asked Gordon.

Chambers smiled.

"How long am I supposed to stay cooped up in this damn place?" asked Rachel Morrison, sitting back against the headboard of the bed, wearing nothing but her faded red sweatshirt and a pair of black lace panties. Her pose was one of calculated, seemingly casual seductiveness, one leg out straight before her, the other bent, attractively at the knee, one hand resting on that knee, holding an unlit cigarette. Her hair was attractively uncombed, partly hanging in her face. It was the look of a wanton trollop, but if she thought she'd get a rise out of Alfred with it, she was very much mistaken.

Alfred had, after all, lived a full life before coming to make his permanent home in Wayne Manor. And during his days at "Rah-Dah," which was how British theater people most commonly referred to the Royal Academy of Dramatic Arts, he'd seen more than his share of attractive, scantily clad, young women. As a younger man, he'd possessed no less charm than he did now, and in his time, he had, as the English would say, "cut quite a swathe among the ladies." He was not easily shocked, nor was he the sort of man whose hormones got the best of him. Quite aside from that, he was old enough to be this young woman's grandfather, and he was, if nothing else, a man of principle and scruples. He did not react to her state of undress at all; instead, he merely took out a cigarette lighter and held it out to her.

"You need not be cooped up in here at all, miss," he replied as she leaned forward toward the lighter with her cigarette. "As you know, if you'd care to go outside into the Batcave, you need only use that phone, as you've just done."

She sighed irritably. "I know *that*," she said. "I mean, how long do I have to *stay* here? Besides, those damn bats give me the creeps."

"They're actually quite harmless, miss," said Alfred, whom she knew only as "Mr. Jones," the cover identity he was using with her in his disguise. He also disguised his voice in speaking with her, using a flawless Boston accent. "In fact, they're very beneficial creatures. As to the duration of your stay here, I should imagine that depends on when they schedule the trial for General Garcia. It's really for your own safety, you know."

"Why do you do that?" she asked suddenly, and Alfred was a bit taken aback by the apparent non sequitur.

"Do what, miss?"

"Call me 'miss,' for one thing. And light my cigarette. I *do* have a lighter, you know."

"Well, quite aside from the fact that smoking is a highly unhealthful practice, though I try not to impose my views on others, I was always taught that it was simple good manners to light a lady's cigarette, or hold a chair for her, or open doors, that sort of thing."

"Why? You think women are helpless?"

"Not at all. I simply believe in treating ladies with respect."

"You do, huh? Would you do those things for a man?"

"Absolutely. The world tends to be a much more pleasant place if people are polite."

She snorted, blowing out a stream of smoke. "God, Jones, you're really something else, you know that?"

"And what would that be?" he asked politely.

"I mean, you walk in here, and I'm practically undressed, and you don't even bat an eye. You just light my cigarette and stand there talking to me as calmly as you please."

"I am not the sort of man to come unglued at the sight of an attractive young women in her unmentionables. Aside from that, I rather doubt you're seriously interested in attempting to seduce me. I think you merely like to shock people sometimes, or demonstrate your nonconformity."

"You do, huh? What makes you think I wouldn't be interested in putting the moves on you?"

"Well, I should think you'd have little trouble in attracting men who were much younger and much more interesting."

She raised her eyebrows. "What if I have a thing for older men?"

"That would be entirely your business," Alfred replied. "I, however, do not have a 'thing' for younger women. Even if I were of that inclination, which I am not, I would never take advantage of a woman in a vulnerable situation."

"You think I'm *vulnerable*? Do I *look* vulnerable to you?"

"You try extremely hard not to," Alfred replied, "but given your efforts, one wonders, as Shakespeare wrote, if the lady 'doth not protest too much'?"

She frowned. "What the hell does *that* mean?"

"Oh, come now, you know very well what it means. You're a remarkably intelligent and articulate young woman, despite your attempts to hide it. I happen to know you studied Shakespeare in college, and did quite well in the course."

"You've seen my college transcript?" she said, astonished.

"Oh, yes. Since we were going to be spending some

time together, I wanted to learn a bit more about you. I know rather more about you than you may think."

She grimaced and exhaled smoke through her nostrils. "Terrific. So you know all about my sordid past. What do you think about it? Not exactly a 'lady,' am I?" she said with exaggerated sarcasm.

"A great many young people make missteps in their youth," Alfred replied. "You've made more than most, to be sure, but despite your involvement with some highly unsavory characters and events, I don't think you're nearly as hardened and cynical as you pretend to be."

"Oh, yeah?" she said.

"*Yeah*," said Alfred, mimicking her.

In spite of herself, she smiled. "Why do I like you, Mr. Jones? If that's really your name, which I'm sure it isn't. I don't like too many people."

"Perhaps because I like *you*," Alfred said. "I have a feeling that not very many people like you. I don't think you make it very easy for them."

She sighed. "Listen... this is going to sound kinda silly, but would you mind turning your back for a minute? I suddenly feel like a jerk sitting here in my underwear, and I'd like to put my pants back on."

Alfred smiled. "Certainly." He turned around.

A moment later, she said, "Okay, you can turn around."

He turned back to face her.

"I guess you think I'm pretty foolish," she said.

"Not at all," said Alfred. "Confused, perhaps, but not foolish. You've done some very foolish things, but what you're doing now is making up for that."

"You think so, huh?" She grimaced and shook her

head. "I don't know. I saw the news about those bombs last night." She paused. "I can't help feeling it was all my fault."

Alfred sat down on the edge of the bed. "You mustn't think that," he said. "You're trying to do the right thing. Perhaps to make up for all the wrong things that you've done. What you are going to do will put General Garcia, and, with any luck, the men behind him, on whose orders those terrible things were done, out of business—permanently."

She shook her head. "You don't know those people, Mr. Jones," she said. "I do."

"You don't know the Batman," Alfred replied. "*I* do."

"You have a lot of faith in him, don't you?" she said.

"I've known him for a very long time," Alfred replied. "And I know that when he sets his mind upon a task, he sees it through, no matter what or who may stand in his way."

"What is it with him?" she asked. "I mean, he's obviously got a lot of money. You can tell that just from looking at the Batcave and all that... that stuff out there. I mean, he's rich, right?"

"Well, let's simply say that money is not really a problem," Alfred replied.

"So why does he do it? I mean, who does he think he is? He got some kinda hero thing, or what?"

"Well, I don't know that I'd refer to it as a 'hero thing,'" said Alfred with a smile, "but there's nothing ignoble in being heroic. You're being heroic in what you're doing, believe it or not. I find that very admirable. As for the Batman, what motivates him is a concern for justice. There is little enough of it in the world today. He's only one man, but he's doing what he can.''

"Why?"

"Well, he has some very personal reasons,'' Alfred replied, "but perhaps more than anything else, he does what he does because he wants to make a difference in the world.''

"He thinks he can change the world?'' she said with a grimace. "Good luck.''

"Luck has a little to do with it,'' Alfred replied, "but primarily, it's perseverance and dedication. He's not unrealistic, you know. He knows one man, no matter how unique that man may be, cannot change the world all by himself. But he can make a difference in it. And if you can make a difference, then in some small way, you *are* changing things, aren't you? Consider yourself. What you're doing is going to make a difference. You are going to testify against General Garcia, and it will result in his conviction, which in turn will result in his no longer being able to disseminate narcotics or provide support to terrorists or abuse his people. And, with any luck, if he makes a deal with the prosecutor in return for consideration in his sentencing, it will help to put the people behind him out of business as well. I'd say that's making quite a difference. No action, no matter how small, is entirely without consequence. Every man and every woman is capable of doing something to make a difference in the world, even if it's only a small difference. However, the sum of those small differences can add up to quite a large result. And if that isn't changing the world, I don't know what is.''

She smiled ruefully. "You're an idealist, Mr. Jones. Just like the Batman. You're living in a dream world."

"I freely admit to being an idealist," said Alfred. "I do not think it is a bad thing to be an idealist. As for living in a dream world, why not for at least some of the time? If you do not dream, then those dreams cannot come true, can they?"

"The world is not a dream, Mr. Jones," she said sadly. "It's a goddamn nightmare. Especially with people like Specter in it."

There was a knock at the door.

"Gee, I wonder who *that* is," she said wryly.

"Come in," Alfred said.

The door opened, and the Batman entered. "I came to see how our guest was doing," he said.

"Our guest is feeling a bit 'cooped up,'" said Alfred. "And somewhat discouraged, I'm afraid."

"I think I know exactly how she feels," the Batman said. He turned to her. "Chin up," he said. "We're making progress."

"Against Specter?" she said skeptically. "You'll never catch him. But sooner or later, he'll catch you."

"That's not exactly what I'd call a vote of confidence," the Batman said.

"Look, don't get me wrong, it's nothing personal," she said. "But you don't know him."

The Batman and Alfred exchanged sharp looks. "You mean .... you *do*?" the Batman said.

She glanced up at him, surprised, caught by her own admission, and looked as if she were about to deny it, then she simply shrugged and said, "We used to be lovers."

"*What?*" the Batman and Alfred said simultaneously. "Why didn't you say anything about this before?" the Batman asked, completely taken aback by her admission.

"What difference would it make?" she said with another shrug.

"*What difference would it make?*" the Batman echoed her. "My God, it could make all the difference in the world! How on earth could you keep something like this to yourself, knowing what's at stake?"

"I'm telling you, it's not going to make the slightest bit of difference," she said bitterly. "Even if he knew I was the government witness against Garcia, he'd still go through with the contract. He's a pro. He prides himself on that."

"Is that all you can think about, *yourself*?" the Batman said furiously. "What about all those people he's killed? Don't they matter to you at all?"

She looked up at him with defiance. "Yes, they matter to me, damn you! You think I was able to get any sleep last night, after seeing what he did on the news? How the hell do you *think* I feel, knowing the man I used to be in love with is capable of doing things like that? And that he's perfectly capable of killing *me* as well, regardless of anything we once had between us? How would *you* feel if you found out that a woman you were in love with was a mass murderer?"

"But... my God," the Batman said, "we know next to nothing about him! You could have helped us!"

She shook her head. "You don't understand. There's nothing I could have told you, or that I *can* tell you, that would be any help to you at all. I don't know anything about the way he works. Even if I told you what he looked like, it wouldn't do any good at all. He won't look the same anymore. He changes his appearance all the time, not only with makeup, but with plastic surgery. The man I knew, and thought I loved, didn't even exist.'' She seemed to collapse into herself. "Besides, if I'd told you that a man like that used to be my lover..." Her voice trailed off.

She was fighting back tears, determined not to cry and failing in the effort. "First Eric, and then Garcia, not to mention all those in between..... Eric probably wasn't even his real name....." She looked up at them, tears streaming from her eyes. She was angry with herself for crying, and at the same time overwhelmed with guilt and misery. "You... you've both been so... so damn *nice*," she said, sobbing. "I can't remember the last time anyone was n-nice to me. And now you hate me, just like all the others!"

"There, there," said Alfred, reaching out to pat her shoulder, but she jerked away from him.

"Don't touch me! She fell back onto the bed, her face turned away from them. "Oh, God, I want to die!"

Alfred stood and looked at the Batman, his face full of concern, and shook his head.

"Rachel...," said the Batman, kneeling by her bed. "Rachel, look at me."

"No! Leave me alone!"

"Rachel Morrison, you *look* at me."

She could not resist that commanding tone. She turned toward him, fearfully.

"Now, *listen* to me," said the Batman firmly. "You've gone through your entire life feeling bitterness, anger, and resentment. And look what it's brought you to. Now,

I'm not going to sit here and hold your hand and tell you that everything is going to be all right, because that's up to you. If you want to change your life, then you're the one who's going to have to take responsibility for it. You've had a hard life, Rachel, but you're not the only one. There are a lot of people who've been hurt. Believe me, I *know*. I've been there. You can wallow in bitterness and remorse and self-pity, and you can hate the world for doing what it's done to you, or you can stand up on your own two feet and make a decision that *you* are going to change things. Because no one else can do it for you. You can help me in ways you probably don't even know. And by God, you *are* going to help me. Because if you don't, then you're no better than *he* is, and whether I hate you or not, whether you're afraid or not, is not the issue." He took her by the shoulders. "The issue is that people are dying out there! So stop feeling sorry for yourself and *help* me! *Please!*"

She blinked back tears and looked into his eyes, seeing the earnest entreaty there. She swallowed hard, took a deep breath, and nodded. "All right," she said, in a small voice. "I'll . . . I'll try."

"Thank you," said the Batman, releasing her. "Now, we'll start at the beginning. When and how did you meet?"

She took a deep breath and lit up another cigarette to steady her nerves. "It was about eight years ago, in East Berlin. . . ."

CHAPTER
NINE

HIS first choice would have been the rock concert that had been scheduled for the Gotham Arena tonight, but unfortunately the promoters had canceled the event at the last minute. The headliners, a heavy-metal band whose lurid album covers depicted violent satanic imagery and whose hoarse-voiced lyrics were replete with references to death, destruction, and dismemberment, had, when confronted with the possibility of the real thing, refused to go on. It was a pity, he thought. A concert hall jam-packed with screaming teenagers... it would have been a splendidly effective demonstration. And in taking out that band, it would have been a public service.

After the destruction of Club 34, he knew that the nightlife in Gotham City could be expected to take a sudden and dramatic downturn. He had been prepared for that. There was no need to blow up another nightclub.

Aside from that, it was too easy. There were plenty of other targets available. He had his next two devices already prepared. However, he still had several hours left before he would have to leave to place them. He fully intended to make good use of that time.

He sat cross-legged on the living-room rug in the apartment. Spread out all around him were photocopies of magazine articles and extensive notes he'd taken while scanning microfiche copies of Gotham City's newspapers. He had spent most of the day in the public library, researching his next hit. Only, this one would not be a contract. This one was for himself.

He had painstakingly researched everything he could find that had been written about the Batman. He did not expect to find any real answers here. The answers were for him to search out. But among the material that he had gathered, he would find the clues that would set him on the right track. He was an expert manhunter himself, after all.

He had briefly looked through the articles that had appeared in the more sensational newspapers, the sort found on racks by the cash registers in supermarkets. Like the British, Americans had two distinctly different types of newspapers. One that could legitimately lay claim to reporting news, and one that catered to the lowest common denominator of public taste. Much of what was written here he could discount as fantasy. "I Was the Batman's Secret Lover!" one headline had read, and the article proceeded to report the claims of an attractive young model, depicted wearing a scanty bikini in a full-page photograph. The Batman allegedly took her to the Batcave, where he made passionate love to her for hours on end in a secluded grotto. Another article was about a custom hot rod designer from Tennessee who claimed that he had actually designed the Batmobile and had been cheated by his cowled client. "The Batman Is an Alien!" blared another headline, with an accompanying "eyewitness testimony" from a housewife in Teaneck, New Jersey, who claimed to have caught a glimpse of the Batman without his mask on and seen a strange network of veins all over his bald head, which had horns on top, covered by the ears of the mask. There was an artist's rendition of what the woman "saw." Other articles went on much in the same vein, all utter nonsense, either the fabrications of reporters or the ravings of pathetic individuals who would say or do anything for attention. Nevertheless, he glanced through them all, for he did not wish to overlook anything.

The mainstream newspapers produced more solid information, as did some of the feature articles in the magazines. Some, such as the paper that aspired to a sort of counterculture status and featured currently fashionable musicians and celebrities on its covers, took a highly critical view of the Batman, while others were supportive and one or two actually attempted to be objective. Clearly, the Batman had not cooperated with any of these journalistic efforts, and much of what was written was little more than speculation. But some facts did emerge, and little by little, they began to add up.

One thing was clear. Whoever the Batman really was, he had access to a great deal of capital. Either he himself was an extremely wealthy man, worth millions, or he had someone very wealthy bankrolling him. There was no solid evidence to support either theory over the other, but he tended to lean toward the former. The Batman was a loner. Clearly an obsessive personality. A strong personality. The Batman did not strike him as someone who would be comfortable being dependent on anyone. A personality like that would insist upon total control, and total control would not be possible with someone else in charge of the purse strings. So he was undoubtedly a wealthy man. That narrowed the focus considerably.

It was highly unlikely that he had a family. He seemed to subscribe to some sort of chivalric moral code, and someone like that would not discount responsibility to loved ones. His exposing himself to danger on a regular basis would not only risk depriving a family of support, but it would make them vulnerable in the event his identity was ever discovered. And unless they knew what he was up to, which would subject them to constant anxiety and stress, he would have to lead a secret life, hiding his nocturnal activities from them. And while that was not impossible, it would complicate his life immensely. No, a man with such a directed personality would not have any room in his life for family affections and responsibilities. It would only constitute a distraction. So, the Batman would have to be single.

Rich. And single. He would also have to live in Gotham City, or somewhere close by. And he would require a base of operations that could be kept secret. The Batcave. The Batman's lair was reportedly located in some hidden cavern. That left out the Gotham City metropolitan area. The ground beneath the city was honeycombed with subway and maintenance tunnels, pipes and conduits for utilities, and huge tunnels dug deep beneath the earth by sandhogs for bringing water to the teeming population of the city. It was possible for a cavern system to exist somewhere beneath all that, but extremely unlikely, both from a geologic standpoint and from the fact that the constant construction and repair that went on in the city would entail too great a risk of its discovery. So the Batcave was somewhere outside the city.

That did not necessarily mean that the Batman himself had to live outside the city. His residence could be in Gotham and the Batcave elsewhere. Yet, again, that would involve further complications. Travel from his residence to the Batcave might be observed. And someone like the Batman, obsessive, directed, and controlled, would pursue caution and efficiency, which strongly suggested that he would make his residence convenient to his base of operations.

So. Rich. And single. And he lived somewhere outside the city, but relatively close by. He would have to be reasonably young and extremely fit. He had the build of a champion athlete, a man who had spent years training with weights and becoming expert in gymnastics and martial arts. The focus became even sharper.

Rich, single, lived outside the city, possibly with a residence in the city as well, reasonably young, and in peak physical condition. That easily eliminated many of the wealthy citizens of Gotham and its environs.

Was it possible for such a man to conceal his wealth? Perhaps. A resourceful man could find ways to do so. He had done it himself. But then, it was easier to conceal the source of one's wealth and the extent of it when one had no fixed abode. Yet the Batman seemed to confine his activities primarily to Gotham City. Secret accounts in

Swiss banks, or in the Cayman Islands, or in Latin America, perhaps? No, again unlikely. It would entail too many complications, too much risk of discovery. It would be necessary to transfer funds somehow, and that would leave a trail that the American IRS would immediately pounce upon. Through elaborate subterfuges, it could still be done, but it would be far simpler and more effective to maintain a more obvious cover, that of some well-known millionaire whose wealth was easily accounted for.

However, that would also attract attention. As he sat and thought, perusing his notes and his research materials, he tried to put himself into the Batman's place. Tried to imagine what sort of personality he was, how he would think, how he would go about covering his tracks. Rich, single, young, extremely fit... all that would make him very prominent. The single women of the city would consider him a "catch." More complications. The Batman was not someone who would allow himself to become entangled in any romantic relationships. Too time-consuming, too distracting, too risky. So what was the alternative? If his public identity was without any sort of personal social life, people would wonder why. The answer seemed obvious. Instead of avoiding a social life, he would have one that was very visible but still did not allow for any entanglements. He would "play the field," as the Americans put it. Be seen with lots of different women, obviously enjoying their company, but enjoying the lifestyle and the variety too much to settle down into a steady relationship with any one of them.

Gotham City had a number of extremely wealthy, bachelor playboys who were young and very fit, all listed in the social register. These days, it seemed that almost everyone worked out, and lean, muscular bodies were not uncommon. However, the Batman's muscular development was well above average, on the Mr. Universe level. The only problem was, even a Mr. Universe did not look like Mr. Universe in clothes. With jackets having padded shoulders, giving the illusion of well-developed deltoids, and current styles featuring loose and comfortable clothing, the Batman could easily "dress down" to deemphasize his muscularity. With unpadded jackets, well-tailored, yet with a loose and casual drape, much could be concealed. He would still look very fit and athletic, but no more so than hundreds of other physically fit males. Still, those criteria reduced the possibilities considerably.

He made a list of all the men in Gotham City who fit the profile. On his return trip to the library, he would go through all the gossip and society columns of the newspapers kept on microfiche, learning more about these men and comparing their activities. He glanced over the list he'd made. One of the names on it was the Batman. He was absolutely certain of it.

"Thought you ought to see this, sir," said Capiletti, coming into Gordon's office. He handed him a hastily scrawled memo. "It just came in over the radio to the Specter task force."

Gordon read the memo

To: Specter Task Force. From: the Batman. Subject: Update on Specter. Re: Physical description. Height: approx. six feet. Weight: approx. 180 lbs. Color hair: pure white. Complexion: pale (albino), sharp features. Age: 39. Distinguishing characteristics: Eyes are extremely pale, almost pink and colorless, due to albinism. May be disguised with contact lenses. Walks with slight limp in left leg, result of old shrapnel wound. Nose slightly crooked from old break. (Note: might have been repaired by plastic surgery.) Subject may be disguised or may have had appearance altered with plastic surgery. Also difficult to disguise extremely pale skin, except with makeup. Watch for color of skin on hands, or possible use of gloves. Subject is right-handed. Normally speaks with Continental accent, origin may be German. Is fluent in English, German, Russian, French, Spanish, and Arabic. Known aliases: Eric Weiss (pronounced "vice"), Hans Sterne (pronounced "shtern"), Devon Stuart, Phillipe Duval, Andre Chalet (pronounced "sha-lay"). One of these may be his real name. Subject is always armed and extremely dangerous. Expert marksman, expert in demolitions and electronics, expert in martial arts. Subject is known to prefer L.A.R. Grizzly Win Mag semiautomatic. Also habitually wears Fairburn-Sykes-style stiletto in sheath strapped to left forearm.

Gordon frowned. "Where the hell did he *get* all this?"

"He didn't say," replied Capiletti. "It went out over the radio to the whole task force, including the citizen observers."

"Does Chambers know about this yet?"

"I don't think so. He's catching some sack time in the captain's office."

"Okay, well, don't wake him. He needs his rest. But make sure he sees this as soon as he wakes up. And make sure this goes out at once as an APB."

"You got it."

"We're going to get you, Specter," Gordon mumbled as Capiletti left to put the information out over the police radio. "We're going to get you."

The evening rush-hour traffic was just starting as Louis Delgado drove his cab toward the Midtown Tunnel. He was just ahead of most of the traffic. It was already starting to get heavy. The mass exodus from Gotham City to the suburbs would have traffic crawling, bumper-to-bumper, on the expressway, and he hated getting caught in that. Usually, he'd drop the taxicab off at the garage, pick up his own car, and make the twenty-minute drive to his home across the river. If he hit the rush-hour traffic, it could take three to four times that long. Then, if he was off that night, he'd have supper with his wife, who would just be getting off work at the restaurant where she waited tables, and settle down to some TV for the night. Or, if money was tight—and it always was—he'd relax for an hour or two and then head back into the city to drive another shift. Tonight, he was taking the cab home, because he was just going to grab some dinner with Maria and then spend his off-duty hours helping out the Batman as part of his citizen observer task force.

He had explained it to Maria and she understood and gave him her full support. She would much rather have spent the time with him. But she did not complain. She was proud that he would be doing something to help try to catch this Specter character, and when she heard that it was for the Batman, she'd simply said, "Hey, babe, if it's for the Batman, *I'll* go out there with you."

But that was out of the question, of course. The point was, when it came to the Batman, Maria was ready to drop everything and lay it on the line. If the Batman had asked her to go away and spend a weekend with him in the Poconos—not that he'd ever do anything like that—she'd go with no questions asked.

Maria wouldn't be alive now if it wasn't for the Batman. It was back when they were still living in the city, right after they got married, and she was coming home one night from working a split shift at the lounge where she was waiting tables. Ordinarily, Louis would have picked her up, because he didn't like her going home alone, but one of the drivers had called in sick and he had to take another shift and, besides, they'd really needed the money. So Maria was walking home alone, heading toward the subway, when it happened. Three guys jumped her. She tried to fight them, but they had knives and they dragged her into an alley, tore her blouse open, yanked down her skirt, and were just about to violate her when the Batman dropped down on them from out of nowhere.

They went at him with their knives, for all the good it did them. Maria later told Louis that it had all happened so fast that she could hardly even see what he had done. It was like a blur of hands and feet, and the next thing she knew, there were three unconscious rapists in the alley—turned out they'd raped and killed over a dozen women—and the Batman was helping her up, speaking to her gently, helping her cover herself up and asking if she was all right. He tied up the three rapists for the police, then took her to this place where a lady doctor named Leslie Thompkins took care of her and made sure she was all right. Those three bastards went away for life, and as far as Maria was concerned, anything the Batman wanted, he got. And that went double for Louis Delgado.

Louis drove his cab into the tunnel and was about halfway through it when he saw a car stalled in the left lane, its emergency flashers blinking and the hood up. The other cars were all going around it, and traffic was starting to back up. With the rush hour getting under way, it was going to cause a real tie-up. Louis pulled around the stalled car, stopped in front of it, and got out. A tall, well-dressed man with white hair and very pale features approached him.

"Got some trouble?" Louis said.

"Yes, I'm afraid so," the man said, speaking with a foreign accent. "Thank you so much for stopping."

"What's the problem?" Louis said, heading toward the front of the stalled car. He frowned. Something was nagging away at the back of his mind.

"I don't know," the man said. "I'm not mechanically inclined, I'm afraid. And there's really no place to push the car out of the way in here. Perhaps you could give me a lift to the end of the tunnel and I could have someone come and tow me out?"

Louis looked inside the engine compartment but could see nothing obviously wrong. He frowned again. What the hell? Something was bugging him, something he ought to be remembering. . . .

"Yeah, I can give you lift, no problem," he said.

"Thank you very much," the man said, heading

toward the cab. He was walking with a slight limp. "You're very kind."

Louis glanced into the stalled car and noticed that the man had left an attaché case on the front seat. "Hey, mister! You forgot your briefcase!"

The man got in on the driver's side of the cab, slipped behind the wheel, and turned the key in the ignition.

"Hey!" shouted Louis.

The cab peeled out as the stranger took off down the tunnel.

"Hey, man! Hey, that's my cab! What the—" Louis suddenly stopped short. He stared at the briefcase on the front seat of the stalled car. And it clicked. *"Madre de Dios!"*

Louis wrenched open the car door and took out the briefcase. Then he ran in front of the traffic slowing down to go around the stalled car. He stopped a car and ran around to the side as the driver rolled down the window.

"Get outta the car, man!" Louis shouted.

"What?"

"Get outta the car!" Louis screamed, wrenching open the door and pulling the driver out with his free hand. *"I got a bomb here!"*

"Jesus Christ..."

Louis jumped into the car and floored it, leaning on the horn all the way as the car shot off down the tunnel. He kept glancing at the case on the front seat beside him. "Oh, don't blow up, man, please, don't blow up! Come on! Come *on*, get outta the way!"

He weaved through the traffic, bouncing off other cars, all his years of driving a cab in Gotham City paying off as he tore through the traffic at a breakneck pace. As he drove, he prayed in Spanish, thinking about Maria, thinking about the baby on the way, pleading with the Blessed Virgin not to let him die....

He shot out of the tunnel and, with tires screeching and horn blaring, turned back toward the river. A police car took off in hot pursuit behind him.

"Oh, man, don't block me off, man," he pleaded as he floored the accelerator. He had to make it to the bridge. He *had* to.

Another police car joined in the pursuit as he approached the bridge. Thankfully, traffic on this side was light. He skidded to a stop in the center of the bridge, and leaped out of the car, holding the case in his hand. Behind him, the police cars screeched to a halt.

"All right, *freeze!*" one of the cops yelled.

"I got a bomb!" Louis shouted as he ran over to the railing and flung the case out over the side as hard as he could. It tumbled down toward the river, but it hadn't even hit the water when the bomb went off with a devastating roar.

"Holy cow!" said one of the cops, lowering his service revolver.

Louis was on his knees, crossing himself and shaking like a leaf as he thanked God for his life. The police officers took his report, about the bomb, about Specter, and about his stolen cab, which was later found abandoned, and they told him that he was a hero. Later that night, he and Maria watched the evening news and Louis saw himself being interviewed about what happened, and Maria, with tears in her eyes, kissed him and told him she was proud of him. "But you ever do *anything* like that again," she said, "I'll freakin' *kill* you!"

And then the phone rang and Maria picked it up. Her eyes grew wide and her jaw fell as she handed the phone to Louis. He heard the caller say, "This is Batman, Louis. I just wanted to tell you that what you did today was an incredibly unselfish act of courage. You're a hero, and I salute you. But you've done more than enough for one man, Louis. You stay home now. I don't want you taking any more chances. You stay home with Maria, with the knowledge that you have my thanks and the gratitude of the people of this city. God bless you."

"Thank you," Louis said. "Thank you very much." Stunned, Louis hung up the phone.

"He remembered my name!" Maria said. "He actually remembered my name!"

"I'll be damned," said Louis. "He called me! The Batman called *me*!"

"That's 'cause you're a hero, babe," said Maria, putting her arms around him and kissing him on the lips. She gave him a slow smile. "Come on, hero. Come to bed."

He clicked the remote control, shutting off the small portable television set he'd purchased earlier that day to replace the one that he'd destroyed in an outburst of fury. He sat there, fuming, staring at the blank screen. That idiot cabdriver had ruined everything. Who would have expected someone like that to play the hero? He was lucky. Lucky he hadn't been blown to bits. But the bomb had gone off without doing any damage. If it had gone off inside the tunnel, in the middle of all that rush-hour traffic... *Damn* it. Now they had a description of him, too. A police artist had made a surprisingly accurate sketch, which they had shown on the newscast. That had been very careless of him. He should have worn a disguise, but he hadn't expected that cabdriver to live long enough to give anyone his description. And the bomb should have gone off earlier. The timing mechanism must have been faulty. He could have used a remote, radio-controlled detonator, but inside the tunnel it never would have worked. And that damned cabdriver never would have interfered if it hadn't been for the Batman.

Again, the Batman. He was starting to become a serious aggravation. That cabdriver never would have made it out of that tunnel alive if he hadn't recognized him. The fact that he *had* recognized him was shocking. He had told the reporters that he had recognized him from a description that the Batman had circulated. The last thing he had expected was that anyone might recognize him. And because of that cabbie's ridiculous heroics, and that faulty timing mechanism, which had been too slow—damned American products—it had all gone wrong. Now he would have to change his face again.... He smashed his fist against the armrest of the chair.

How in God's name had the Batman gotten his description? And where had he circulated it? To whom? To the police, obviously, but apparently also to the cabdrivers. And to who else? Bus drivers? Transit authority police? Hotel and restaurant personnel? It made no difference anyway; thanks to that cabbie, his description was now all over the city. But how had the Batman known in the first place?

He never should have taken this job. He didn't like America, and he didn't like the imprecision of using bombs. He was not a terrorist, he was an assassin. This wholesale slaughter lacked finesse. He could take no satisfaction in it. Any fool could plant a bomb. Stalking a known target and executing the contract in a clean, methodical, skillful, and efficient manner was much more suited to his taste. This . . . this was . . . inconvenient.

It was also frustrating. And the Batman's interference was galling. It was humiliating. He was a professional, at the very top of his craft, and this ludicrous, melodramatic clown in a masquerade costume was getting in his way. Inconvenient, indeed. It was past time to do something about this inconvenience.

He still had to plant the second bomb, but that could wait a few hours. He was feeling highly irritable, and he needed to calm down. This would never do. He took pride in the coolly dispassionate and calculated way in which he always worked, and this level of anger and frustration was something he was not accustomed to. He needed to remove the source of it. He needed to teach this Batman a lesson. A permanent lesson. And it would also serve the purpose of his mission, not only by restoring him to clarity, but by demonstrating to the people of Gotham City that he was the master of their celebrated "caped crusader." In Gotham City, the Batman was like an icon. He would destroy that icon, and demoralize these people.

He started once more looking through his research materials, the exhaustive notes he'd taken in the library, the clippings of newspaper and magazine articles. Now he was looking to learn as much as possible about the wealthy, young, male citizens of Gotham City who fit the Batman's profile. A number of them he was quickly able to cross off his list. Others took a little while longer. The hours stretched as he worked at his task. Eventually, he was down to only a couple of names. Billionaire David Jacks and playboy industrialist Bruce Wayne.

One of these two men was the Batman. He felt certain of it. But which one? He tossed his notes aside and lit up one of his French cigarettes. It made no difference. He would kill them both.

CHAPTER
TEN

"YOU haven't touched your dinner," she said, looking at the tray Alfred had left for him.

The Batman glanced away from the computer screen. "Rachel. I'm sorry, I didn't hear you come in. I must have been distracted."

"I said you haven't eaten anything," she said.

"I've been too busy."

"Looking for Eric."

"Yes. Or whatever his name really is. I don't really care at this point. I only want to find him and stop him. Keep him from hurting any more people." He turned back to the screen.

"He used to call me that too."

"What?"

"Eric. Specter. Whoever he is. He called me Rachel. Everyone else always called me Ray. He said it wasn't feminine." She grimaced. "You call me Rachel too."

"It's a nice name, Rachel."

"Maybe. But I'm not a very nice person, am I?"

"You're not locked into that, you know. You're free to change."

"How do you change once you've been a terrorist?"

"If you're looking for absolution, Rachel, I'm not the man you want to see," he said while staring at the computer screen. "I'm not a priest."

"I don't have much use for priests," she replied. "Or for organized religion."

"That's entirely your business. I wasn't trying to turn this into a discussion on religion. My point is simply that there is no avoiding the responsibility for what you've done with your life, at least not for an ethical person. However, that doesn't mean you're trapped by what you've done or what you've been. You say you've never killed anyone, and I believe you. It's one thing to engage in training-camp maneuvers with live ammo and provide logistical support for terrorists, and it's quite another to actually kill people yourself. I'm not excusing what you did. I don't think it doesn't make you guilty. It's simply a lesser degree of guilt. But you can accept that guilt and change."

"Can I? I wish I could believe that."

"Believe it. History is full of people who've done far worse things than you have and turned it all around. Criminals *can* be rehabilitated. A jail term by itself isn't going to do that. All prison can do is remove you from society so you can no longer endanger anyone, and give you time to think. What you do with that time is entirely up to you. Some criminals use it to become more embittered and learn how to be better criminals. Others use it to reexamine their lives and look for ways to live them more constructively. You're lucky. You won't be going to prison. You're going to get a chance to start all over again, with a new identity. It's still not going to absolve you of everything you've done, though. It's merely a second chance. A chance to change. What you do with it is up to you."

"One thing about you," she said, "you sure don't pull any punches, do you?"

"What would be the point? If you have respect for people, Rachel, then you're truthful with them."

"You can respect *me*?"

"What you're doing is worthy of respect."

She grimaced. "Is it? The only reason I did it is that I wanted out, away from Garcia. I didn't do it because I was trying to do good, I did it because I was tired of being a toy for every militant extremist who came down the pike. I just wanted to go home."

"The motives for doing a good thing aren't as important as the fact that the good thing gets done," the Batman said. "If your only motive was self-preservation, then there's nothing wrong with that, if some good comes out of it. And if you've learned from the experience."

"I wouldn't have figured you for the nonjudgmental type," she said.

"I'm not," the Batman replied. "I don't think anyone really is. But if you're looking for me to blame you, then you're barking up the wrong tree. You're the one who's doing the blaming. You're blaming yourself. That's just a part of working through your guilt. Before you can get past it, you first have to accept it. And then you have to work on forgiving yourself, because no one else can do it for you. However, the fact that you can feel the guilt means there's hope for you. When it starts eating away at you, remember that."

"You're an unusual man," she said, gently putting her hand on his shoulder.

The Batman smiled. "I've been told that."

"I wish I could see what you look like behind that mask."

"I'm afraid that's a wish that I can't grant you," he replied.

"Have you ever granted it to any woman?"

"Not in the sense I think you mean, no."

"So . . . there's never been anybody . . . special?"

"A lot of people are special to me, Rachel."

"You know what I mean." Her fingers trailed down his arm.

He punched some keys on the computer, halting the flow of data, and looked up at her. "Yes, I know what you mean. And the answer to that is no. Not because I want it that way, but because that's the way it has to be."

"Don't you ever get, you know, lonely?"

"Yes. I'm only human."

"A man has physical needs."

"Physical needs can be sublimated," he replied. "Emotional needs are not so easy, but I find many of my emotional needs filled by what I do."

"But not all?"

"No. Not all."

"It doesn't have to be that way."

He met her gaze. "Yes, Rachel. It has to be."

She moistened her lips nervously. "What I'm trying to say is, I mean, if you find me attractive . . ."

He smiled. "I know what you're trying to say. And I appreciate it. Really. I meant what I said. I'm not rejecting you, but it's unfair to become involved with someone without being able to offer them some kind of emotional commitment. And you already know what it's like to be involved with someone who can't or won't do that. I can't do what you're suggesting without becoming emotionally involved. And that's something I simply cannot afford. Aside from that, you really don't know anything about me."

"I know all I need to know."

"No," he said, gently, "you don't. You really don't."

She looked away. "Is it because of who...what I am?"

"No. It's because of who and what *I* am."

She smiled ruefully. "Well, it's been a long time since I've been turned down."

"I'm not turning you down," the Batman said. "I'm turning *me* down. The loss is mine, believe me."

She pursed her lips and slowly shook her head. "No, it's not." She sighed. "I'm sorry, I didn't mean to interrupt your work."

"It's all right," he said, turning back to the computer screen. He punched some keys, and the data flow resumed.

"Am I in your way?"

"No, not really."

"What is that you're looking at?"

"Phone-company work orders," he replied. "What I'm trying to do is...Wait a minute...."

He punched some keys and stopped the flow of data once again. He split the screen and compared what he was looking at to a display of several other files.

"What is it?" Rachel asked.

"Records for an apartment in the Village," he replied, "one of the list of those in the ads for temporary subletters. The phone service was disconnected two weeks ago, and it hasn't been reestablished, but according to public service, the tenant is still using the gas and electricity. And, according to the classified records of the *Gotham Voice,* the ad for that apartment was pulled when it still had a week to run, which indicates that the apartment was sublet."

"Maybe they just didn't pay their phone bill," she suggested.

"No, there's a voluntary disconnect order, with a note that service will be reestablished in six months, so that the number won't be assigned to anybody else. That means the old tenants will return in six months and they still want to keep the same number. They just disconnected service so the subletter wouldn't run up their phone bill and could reestablish service temporarily, with a different number in his own account. Only, he hasn't done that. As for the utilities, they've probably worked that into the rent."

"So what does that mean?"

"It means that whoever is subletting this apartment doesn't want a phone," the Batman said. "And while that's not unheard of, it's certainly unusual. Let's see what we can learn about the original tenants. There's two of them listed here...."

He ran a check on them through public-service and phone-company records, as well as their social security numbers.

"Professional musicians," he said. "And if they're

musicians and they live in the Village, then they undoubtedly shop at Ballardi's Music Center." He checked the time. "It's almost nine-thirty. And Gene stays open late, so there's still a chance...." He grabbed the phone, checked his computerized directory, and punched out a number.

A querelous voice answered, "Ballardi's. We're closed."

The Batman smiled. Some businesses never answered the phone after closing, but if Gene was still in, he always did, on the chance that some rich rock star needed a new guitar in a hurry. "Gene, it's the Batman."

"No kiddin', *really*?"

"Yes, really. How's your shoulder?"

"All healed up now. And the bastards that shot me are still in jail, thanks to you. I recognize your voice now. I was just closing out the register. Hell, what can I do for ya, buddy?"

"I'm not sure if you can help me, Gene, but I'm trying to run down a couple of musicians who live in your area."

"Shoot."

"Their names are David Stoner and Richard—possibly Rick or Dick—Lee."

"Oh, yeah, sure. I know those guys. They play in a band called the Dogs. Why, they haven't done anything, have they?"

"No, I'm sure they haven't, but I need to find out if there's any way that I can get in touch with them. It's important."

"Hell, I don't know, they're out on tour. Wait a minute, lemme see what I can do here. Hold on a sec..." There was a brief pause during which the

Batman could hear papers rustling in the background as Gene went through the usual pile of debris on his cluttered desk, searching for his Rolodex. "Ah, here we go. They're with Daystar Management. Their office will be closed now, but I might be able to get a hold of Shelley.... Want I should try him at home?"

"Yes, please, could you do that, Gene?" said the Batman. "I need to speak to them tonight, if it's at all possible."

"Okay, I'll see what I can do. Give me about five minutes and then call me back."

"Will do," the Batman said. "And thank you, Gene. I really appreciate this."

"Hey, no problem. I owe ya, big fella. Talk to ya in a bit."

He hung up the phone.

"I'm impressed," said Rachel. "I'd hate to be the one trying to hide from *you*."

"It could still be a false lead," said the Batman, "but my gut instinct is telling me we may be on the right track. I only hope I can get through to those musicians tonight."

Slightly over five minutes later, he called the music-store owner back.

"Okay," said Gene, "the tour's in Denver. It's about eight o'clock in Colorado right now, and they're not due to start playing till about nine, so you might still catch them at the hotel. Here's the room number...."

Several moments later, he had a disbelieving David Stoner on the phone, the lead guitarist for the Dogs. "This is a joke, right?" Stoner said. "Who is this, really?"

"It's no joke, Mr. Stoner, I assure you," said the Batman. And he explained about Gene and how he was able to track them down. "What you tell me could be of the gravest importance, Mr. Stoner, in trying to track down a ruthless crimninal. What can you tell me about the person who is subletting your apartment?"

"Devon Stuart? He's with a movie company from England. Least that's what he said. He told us he was—"

"Did you say *Devon Stuart?*"

"Yeah, that's right."

"Can you describe him?"

"Sure. Late thirties, early forties, white hair, pale, what they call an albino. Very hip dude, sharp dresser, speaks with an accent, walks with a limp—"

"Thank you very much, Mr. Stoner," said the Batman, interrupting him. "You've been extremely helpful."

"Hey, no problem," Stoner said. "Why, what's he done?" But the phone had already gone dead.

David Jacks came out of his bedroom wearing a dark-blue silk dressing gown. His hair was mussed and he was barefoot. Behind him, through the open bedroom door, a young woman's voice called out, "David?"

"I'll be right there, babe," he called out. He went over to the bar to make himself a drink.

"Where's your costume tonight?" an accented voice asked.

Jacks glanced up, startled. "Who the hell are *you? How did you get in here?*"

The white-haired man shook his head. "No, you're not the one, are you? Pity."

"What the hell are you talking about? Who *are* you?" Jacks reached for the phone. "I'm calling security."

"I think not, Mr. Jacks." The silenced Grizzly coughed three times.

"David? David? Who are you talking to?"

An attractive and shapely young blond woman came to the bedroom door, a sheet wrapped around her. She saw Jacks' body on the floor, and she saw the stranger with the big gun, and she opened her mouth to scream....

Specter fired.

How very unfortunate, he thought as he rode back down to the lobby in Jacks' private elevator. In his left hand, he held an attaché case. Well, it didn't matter much in either case. At least he now knew who the Batman was. It wasn't Jacks. It was Bruce Wayne. Out of all the candidates, Wayne seemed the least likely suspect. The jaded, dissipated playboy industrialist. Likable and charming, but superficial, shallow, none too bright, and rather irresponsible. A man who delegated all the responsibilities of his life to others so that he could live the uncomplicated life of a pampered hedonist. The man who always had the latest rising young starlet on his arm, or some prominent debutante or nightclub singer. The man who was Gotham City's best known playboy. And yet it fit. It fit perfectly.

What better cover could he have chosen? And he lived just outside the city, on the secluded estate known as Wayne Manor, beneath which, undoubtedly, could be found the Batcave. It was absolutely perfect. Why hadn't he seen it earlier? Because the disguise was so completely realized, because Bruce Wayne was so highly visible, and so obviously the classic example of the decadent

210 / **SIMON HAWKE**

American capitalist who had never truly had to work for anything in his pampered life....

"Oh, you're good, my friend," Specter said to himself as he stepped out of the private elevator, "you're very good indeed. Only, I'm better."

The Batman was, after all, an amateur. A remarkably gifted amateur, but an amateur nonetheless. And he was a pro. He glanced down briefly at the body of the security guard behind the front desk in the lobby and then causally strolled out the door and into the night.

First, he would plant the bomb, timed to explode during the morning commuter rush hour, and then he would see to the elimination of Bruce Wayne. Then, in the morning, confronted with yet another dramatic example of what continued resistance would mean for the people of Gotham City, as well as the demise of their celebrated "caped crusader," along with the witness he had been protecting, the American authorities would have no choice but to cave in and put Garcia on a plane to Cuba, where he would be killed for having made a mess of everything. However, that would not concern him. By then, he'd be relaxing on the deck of a yacht in Monte Carlo, enjoying the fruits of his labors. After this, he thought, perhaps he would retire. Why not? He'd earned it.

They looked like modern pirates in their black silk jackets—embroidered on the backs with coiled green dragons and Chinese characters—their head scarves, earrings, long black hair, and studded wristbands. Their well-faded jeans were ripped at the knees and their high-top basketball shoes were, contrary to fashion, tightly laced in the event that they would have to run or use their feet to deliver kicks. They looked like gang members, and in a sense they were, except that their "gang" was not the sort of street gang the citizens of Gotham City had learned to fear. They were members of the Green Dragons, and the honest citizens of Gotham City had nothing to fear from them. In fact, they had learned to breathe easier anytime they saw Green Dragons sharing a subway car with them, because that meant there were no muggings or assaults.

The transit cop who passed them as they lounged against the wall of Gotham Central Station gave them a sour look. The Gotham City Transit Authority police were not fond of the Green Dragons. They considered them troublemakers and vigilantes. The simple fact was that the Green Dragons were much more effective at crime prevention than were the transit authority cops. But then, perhaps that was because every time some tough-looking characters came aboard a subway car at a stop, the Green Dragons did not get off or move on to another car. They simply stood there, giving the toughs the once-over, with a steady and unblinking gaze that clearly communicated their intent. Ride the subway, fine. Step out of line and we'll step on you. *Hard*. That steady gaze was usually enough to ensure that questionable types quickly got off at the next stop.

The Green Dragons didn't often have to prove themselves. In the beginning, after they were first organized by David Chan, a first-generation Chinese-American who became concerned about the crime in his neighborhood and decided to do something about it, the Dragons did, indeed, have to prove themselves. But David Chan made sure that they were ready for the test. Every single member of the Dragons studied at Sensei Sato's dojo, and every single one of them was adept at hand-to-hand combat and the use of martial-arts weapons, though for the sake of community relations, they carried no such weapons with them when they went out on patrol. In Gotham City, most martial-arts weapons—such as the nunchaku and the shuriken, or throwing stars—were legally classified as lethal weapons, and the penalties for carrying them were the same as for carrying a gun. Consequently, the Green Dragons were usually at risk in what they did, for while they were forced to abide by the city's laws, those whom they confronted usually had no such compunctions.

In this case, their instructions, which had come from Sensei Sato himself, had been very clear. They were not to get involved directly. They were only to watch and to report anything suspicious to the Specter task force at police headquarters. This did not sit well with many of them. It did not sit well with these two, Bobby Wing and Rico Martinez. Bobby, like many of the Dragons, was of Chinese-American descent. Rico's parents had come from San Juan. Both boys were nineteen years old. Both were slim and wiry, as nimble as gazelles and as flexible as snakes. Both of them were confident in their abilities, though neither of them was cocky. If one was cocky when he came to Sensei Sato, he did not stay that way for long. Sato had his own ways of bringing home reality.

Just the same, playing an essentially passive role did not suit these boys very well. They would dearly have loved to get their hands on Specter and use him for a kicking bag. As they stood lounging against the wall, watching everyone who passed, Rico placed a cigarette between his lips. He did not smoke—none of the Dragons did—but he liked to hold one between his lips. He liked the look it gave him. And, coupled with his dark wraparound sunglasses, it did give him a dangerous aspect. He nodded as Shayla, a young black girl also wearing the colors of the Dragons, approached them. She wore a green beret—complete with the Special Forces flash and badge—tight jeans, short, flat-heeled black boots, and a black T-shirt.

"Anything?" she said, tapping her two-way radio lightly against her leg.

"Nah," said Rico. "Same old, same old."

"You guys been keepin' your eyes open?"

"No," said Rico with a wry grimace, "we're just standing here rating all the chicks as they go by. You get a five."

"A *five*?"

"Yeah. That's passing. Barely."

"How'd you like a roundhouse kick upside your head?"

"You two sound like an old married couple," said Bobby with a grin.

"I don't know about the marriage part, but I wouldn't mind the honeymoon," said Rico, grinning back.

"What, with only a five?" said Shayla.

"Okay, six," said Rico.

"Six, my ass," said Shayla. "Honey, I'm a ten, only you can't count that high."

"What time is it?" asked Bobby.

Rico glanced at his watch. "Gettin' up on eleven."

"Man, the night's draggin'," Bobby said. "Figure we

should move around a bit? Check out the platforms? Or do you want to finish your cigarette first?"

"Very funny."

"One of these days, someone'll light that thing for you and you'll cough your lungs out."

"I wouldn't smoke it, man, it's just a prop."

"A prop. Man, you're somethin' else. I don't know what, though."

"You ask me, this is a waste of time," said Rico. "Specter ain't gonna show up here, man. There ain't enough people here this time of night to take out with a bomb. We're not doin' any good here."

"This is our post, and this is where we're gonna stay until we get relieved," said Bobby. "Unless you wanna argue with Sensei. Or the Batman, for that matter."

"I never knew Sensei was tight with the Batman," Shayla said. "Wouldn't it be something to see the two of them spar? Who do you think would win?"

"Hey, no contest," Rico said. "Sensei would wipe him out."

"I don't know," said Bobby. "I hear the Batman's pretty bad."

"Better than Sensei?" Rico said. "No way, man. Sensei's forgotten more moves than the Batman ever learned."

"It sure would be something to see, though," Bobby said.

"Hey, guys," said Shayla, "don't look now, but aren't we supposed to be on the lookout for a guy with a limp?"

They glanced in the direction she was looking, suddenly alert. A man who looked like a homeless derelict passed them, dressed in a long, shabby, wool overcoat that looked like something he'd picked out of the garbage. He was wearing a battered old hat, and his shaggy white hair stuck out from underneath it. The lower part of his face was swaddled in a long and dirty scarf. He seemed to be holding something underneath his coat, with his hands clasped protectively to it, against his chest.

"It's just a bum," said Rico, dismissing him.

"Yeah?" said Bobby. "Did you check out the shoes?"

"The shoes?" said Rico.

"Yeah, the shoes. Since when do bums wear two-hundred-dollar Italian shoes, man?"

"Two-hundred-dollar Italian shoes? How the hell do you know?"

"I know my clothes, man," Bobby said. "Not everybody shops in thrift stores, like you do. I can tell an Armani jacket from a block away, and I know Guccis when I see 'em."

"So maybe somebody threw 'em away."

"*Nobody* throws away Guccis, man. Besides, they looked brand new to me. Still had a shine on 'em. And that 'bum' looked pretty pale, from what I could see of his face. Didn't the sheet say he was an albino?"

"Yeah," Shayla said, "it did. And he was holdin' something under his coat."

"I think we better check this out," said Bobby, moving away from the wall.

"Don't get too close," said Shayla.

"What if it ain't him?" asked Rico, tossing away his unlit cigarette.

"Then we wind up followin' a bum with two-hundred-dollar shoes," said Bobby.

"What if it *is* him?" asked Shayla nervously.

"Then we do exactly what Sensei said," Bobby replied. "We watch and see what he does, then if anything looks weird, we call in."

"A bum with two-hundred-dollar shoes looks pretty weird to me," said Rico.

"Yeah, me too," said Bobby.

The bum glanced back at them over his shoulder. Bobby gave Rico a shot in the shoulder, laughed, then put his arm around Shayla. He started talking loudly, joking with Rico. The bum seemed to dismiss them.

"Don't follow too close," said Bobby. "If this is the guy, then he's pro, man, and we're way out of league."

"Yeah? I'd like to see just how good he is," said Rico.

"If you're not careful, you're liable to find out," Bobby replied, keeping his voice low. "Just don't blow it, man. Stay cool. Shayla, stick the damn radio in your pocket before he sees it."

"What for? It looks just like a regular radio."

"Then make like you're listenin' to it or something. And don't look like you're watching him. Hang back."

They followed him down the escalator to one of the main platforms. At this hour, the escalator was turned off, so they had to use it just like regular stairs. They allowed him to get well ahead of them.

"Don't lose him," Rico said.

"Take it easy," Bobby said. "Where's he gonna go? Down there, the only way out is at the other end of the platform. Don't crowd him."

They got down to the platform and hung back by one of the support columns, acting as if they were talking and joking with each other, waiting for a train. The bum was almost at the other end of the platform. For a moment, he was lost to their sight, then they saw him again, moving toward the far end of the platform. He appeared to be walking more quickly.

"Hey, there he goes," said Rico.

"Don't rush it, man," said Bobby.

"Come on! We'll lose him!"

They started heading quickly toward the other end of the platform. At the top of the stairs, they looked around for a moment. There was no sign of the bum.

"Damn! We lost him!" Rico said.

"Wait a minute, there he is," said Shayla, pointing.

"Don't point, you twit!" said Bobby. "Come on."

They followed in the direction he had gone. He was already lost to their sight. They started moving faster. Then, on the stairs leading back up to the street, they found the discarded overcoat he had been wearing, along with the battered hat.

"What the hell?" said Rico.

"Wait a minute," Bobby said.

"Come on, man, he's just ahead of us!" said Rico, starting up the stairs.

"I said *wait* a minute!" Bobby called out to him. Rico paused.

"What's with you, man?"

"Why would he just go down there on the platform and then go back out again?"

Rico simply stared at him. "You don't think..."

"You know what that place is like during rush hour in

the morning, with all the commuters comin' in?" asked Bobby.

"Oh, man..." said Shayla. "I'm callin' it in."

"Wait a minute," Bobby said. "We'd better make sure. Come on."

They ran back down to the platform.

"What the hell are we lookin' for?" Rico asked.

"Anything that looks like it might have a bomb in it," said Bobby. "A briefcase, a bag of some kind, I don't know, just check everywhere down here...."

They began to search the platform. They looked in all the trash containers, between the candy machines, underneath the benches, everywhere. They couldn't find anything.

"Man, there's nothing here," said Rico.

"There has to be," Bobby insisted.

"We checked everyplace."

Bobby stood still for a moment, thinking, his lips compressed in a tight grimace. "The guy's a pro, man. He wouldn't just stick a bomb where anyone could see it."

"Assuming it was him," said Rico.

"Yeah, right," said Bobby. "A bum with two-hundred-dollar shoes who throws away his overcoat. You ever hear of anything like that, dork?"

"No, guess not."

'Yeah, you guess not. Now come on, *think!* It's *gotta* be down here someplace. If you were gonna plant a bomb down here, where would you put it, so nobody would find it between now and morning?"

Rico bit his lower lip, thinking.

"The tracks!" said Shayla.

Rico and Bobby both stared at her.

"Shit!" said Bobby. "Forget it, babe, you're not a ten, you're a damned *fifty*."

They jumped down onto the tracks.

"Man, what if a train comes?" Rico said.

"Then we see how high you can jump," Bobby said. "Now check where he was standing when we lost sight of him back there."

They moved off down the tracks, scanning the area around them carefully, keeping an ear open for any trains coming down the tunnel.

"I don't see anything," Rico said.

"Keep looking," Bobby said.

The platform was completely deserted. It was eerily quiet.

"There!" said Shayla. "What's that?"

She was bent over, looking underneath the lip of the subway platform. Tucked in underneath it, pushed back into the shadows, among the litter, was an attaché case.

"*Bingo!*" Bobby said.

"Oh, *man* . . ." said Rico.

"Get on the horn, girl," Bobby said. "We just found ourselves a God damn bomb."

He came down from the roof, using a line to rappel down the side of the building. He didn't want to risk making any noise on the fire escape that might give him away. With his dark cape, he blended in with the darkness of the building. He came down without a sound, moving with the lithe grace of a cat until he reached the window of the apartment he was looking for. He hooked a leg over the fire escape, taking care not to make the slightest sound, and listened intently. There seemed to be no sound coming from within.

It was a simple matter to slip the window latch. He reached into his utility belt and carefully squirted a tube of graphite lubricant all around the window, then slowly, with great care, opened it without a sound. The apartment was dark as the Batman stepped inside, every sense on the alert.

There was no one home. Specter was out for the evening. Somewhere, tonight, he was planting another of his devilish bombs. More people would die, unless...

The Batman shined his miniature flashlight all around the apartment. Nothing appeared out of the ordinary in this room. Tensely, he moved into the next room... and froze.

Spread out all over the floor were notes and newspapers and clippings from magazine articles. He crouched down to examine them. It only took a second for him to realize what they were all about. Specter had been researching him just as he had been researching Specter. Stalking him. Trying to discover who he was. The Batman quickly looked through the notes spread out on the floor, then his gaze fell on a sheet of paper with a list of names written on it. They were names of wealthy, young, male citizens of Gotham. Most of the names on the list had been crossed off with a single line through them. But two had not been. Two of the names had been underlined and circled. The names of David Jacks and Bruce Wayne.

"Oh, Lord..." the Batman said. He unclipped the radio from his belt and contacted the task force. "This is the Batman. Priority signal, over."

"*Batman!*" the voice of a police radio dispatcher came back. "We just got a call from the Green Dragons. They saw him! They found a bomb in Gotham Central Station.

We've just dispatched the bomb squad. Have you got anything, over?"

Under other circumstances, the Batman might have sighed with relief, but they were not out of the woods yet. "Yes. Listen carefully. I've found where Specter is staying." He gave the address. "Get some people over here right away to set up an ambush if he comes back. And get a SWAT team over to David Jacks' penthouse right away. I have reason to believe he may be Specter's target. Have you got that, over?"

"Got it. Where will you be, over?"

"Batman, over and out," he said, turning off the radio and clipping it back on his belt. He bolted for the window. He had no time to lose. If he was lucky, then the SWAT team would intercept Specter at Jacks' residence. If not, then Specter was heading straight for Wayne Manor.

CHAPTER
ELEVEN

THE security around the estate was impressive. He had left the stolen car behind and approached on foot, carefully checking out the lay of the land. This was much more to his liking. No sloppy bombs to plant, no dramatic threats to phone in, just a simple job of hunting down his quarry. It was what he was best at. He was in his element.

The gates were controlled electronically, and there were security cameras surmounting them. There was an intercom by the gates. The perimeter of the estate was fenced, but he could see no cameras. At least, not in any obvious locations. And the fence did not look difficult to scale. It was probably wired with an alarm system. Or perhaps there were ground sensors. No, they would be on the inside of the fence, not on the outside. And if there were any ground sensors, or perimeter alarms, they would not be on the drive leading up to the house, which was liable to be covered by cameras. Bruce Wayne was obviously very serious about his security. Of course, he would have to be, since he was the Batman.

The fence would not likely be electrified, although that was possible. But the Batman wouldn't want to injure anyone unnecessarily. So, probably it was just wired with an alarm system. A careful examination soon revealed it. It was carefully concealed, and anyone but a professional would not have spotted it. It was a simple matter to bridge the alarm wires and cut off a section of the fence, which then allowed him to scale it. Once on the other side, he kept close to the fence, moving along it toward the main drive up to the house. He spotted the cameras covering the driveway, concealed behind shrubbery. He smiled. As he had suspected, Wayne was a gifted amateur, but an amateur nonetheless. He used the shrubbery along the driveway for concealment, his black clothing blending in with the darkness, his pale face and white hair concealed by a black nylon balaclava mask. He stayed low, hugging the shrubbery, often moving through it whenever he came near the cameras, keeping out of their line of sight. It was slow going, but he eventually reached the house.

The windows would probably all be wired. So he wouldn't use a window. He would use the front door. There was a camera mounted above the door, cleverly concealed, but it didn't take him long to spot it. At this point, he would take a risk. What were the chances of anyone inside watching the monitors at this hour? Slim. Wayne did not have a large household staff. There was only one butler, an elderly man named Alfred Pennyworth, but still not a man to be dismissed lightly.

Pennyworth might be an old man, but he had served in the S.A.S., and that meant he'd had commando training. So, Pennyworth might be old, but he should not be underestimated.

With just one man on his personal staff—undoubtedly, Pennyworth was in on the secret of his identity as the Batman—Wayne would have most of his security systems automated, as he had seen so far. And automated systems were not difficult to defeat or bypass. If there was no one available to constantly monitor the screens, then there had to be some sort of alarm to serve as an alert. He carefully examined the area around the front door. His gaze fell on the rubber doormat just in front of the door. A very plain rubber doormat. Someone like Wayne might be expected to have something fancier, more ornate, with his name on it. But this one did not attract any attention whatsoever. And, by not attracting any attention, it attracted his attention. He carefully bent down and lifted a corner of it, exposing a pressure plate beneath. He smiled.

Avoiding stepping on the pressure plate beneath the mat, he positioned himself awkwardly, but so that he could work on the lock of the front door. This put him directly in line with the surveillance camera, but he was gambling that at this hour, Pennyworth would be otherwise occupied. In moments, he had smoothly picked the lock and slipped the deadbolt. He tried the door, very gently. It opened without a sound. That made perfect sense, of course. A proper British butler would not suffer a front door to squeak.

He stood in the darkened foyer, listening intently. The house was quiet. He slipped off the balaclava mask and took off his jacket, revealing the shoulder holster worn over his black turtleneck shirt. He carefully hung the jacket over the umbrella stand and moved inside, stepping softly, without making a sound. Wayne certainly lived well, no question about it. And he had exquisite taste. Everything around him spoke of "old money." The grandfather clock standing in the foyer was a nearly priceless antique.

As he moved stealthily through the house, he saw that there was light coming from the kitchen. He approached cautiously. Peering around the corner, he saw a bearded man in his shirtsleeves, preparing a tray with tea and crumpets. He moved about the kitchen as if he was perfectly at home. Obviously, Pennyworth.

He carefully peeked out into the kitchen once again. The butler seemed oblivious of his presence. He finished preparing the tray, then slipped on a tweed sport coat, took out a small pocket mirror and checked his appearance, particularly the hair and beard. Odd. Now why would he and then it struck him. Of course. The witness. Pennyworth would not want the witness to be able to recognize him, because that could tie him into Wayne. So he was wearing a disguise. And it was a very good one.

Specter unholstered the Grizzly. Then Pennyworth did an odd thing. He opened the refrigerator, fiddled with something inside, closed the door and stepped back to pick up the tray. Then there was a whining sort of sound and the entire refrigerator started to retract into the wall.

Well, well, he thought. What have we here?

It was obvious. A concealed entrance to the Batcave. That was a stroke of luck. He would not need to torture

Pennyworth into showing it to him. Pennyworth had obligingly revealed it. And doubtless, he was taking a bedtime snack down to the witness. Tea and crumpets. How quaint. And where was Wayne while all this domesticity was going on? Out chasing him, no doubt. Chasing shadows. Trying to catch a ghost. A Specter. What a surprise the Batman would have waiting for him when he returned.

Pennyworth disappeared with the tray inside the opening left by the retracted refrigerator. Specter moved into the kitchen holding the gun ready. He looked inside the opening. A small elevator shaft. The elevator was descending. He looked down into the opening and he could see the elevator below him, going down. He found the elevator buttons. He would give Pennyworth a few minutes, then summon the elevator back up. And then he would go down and see the Batcave. It was bound to be interesting. It was almost a shame, he thought. It was all so easy. He would first dispose of Pennyworth, and then the witness. Or perhaps he would keep Pennyworth and the witness alive until Wayne returned. Yes, that would be better. It would make him more pliable. And it would draw the affair out pleasantly. First he would shoot him in the right kneecap. Then the left. And then he would make him crawl. And watch helplessly while he killed Pennyworth and blew out the brains of the helpless witness. After that ... well, they would have all night.

He had waited long enough. He summoned the elevator.

"I thought you might care for a bit of refreshment, my dear," said Alfred.

Rachel looked up at him and smiled. "That's sweet of you, Mr. Jones, but I'm not really hungry right now. Maybe later." She was stretched out on the bed, watching a movie on television. It was *Day of the Jackal*. She turned it off with the remote control.

"I didn't mean to interrupt your viewing," Alfred said, setting down the tray.

She made a face. "Not really my kind of film," she said. "A bit too close to home."

"Ah. Well, perhaps you'd care to take a stroll?"

"I thought you'd never ask. I'm starting to go stir crazy in here. Could we go look at the trophy room again?"

"Certainly," said Alfred, with a smile. He held the door open for her. "After you."

"Why, thank you, sir," she said. She chuckled. "You're spoiling me, Mr. Jones. I'm not used to being treated like a lady."

Alfred stepped out into the corridor behind her, then frowned.

"What is it?" she asked. "Something I said?"

"No," said Alfred, still frowning as he looked down toward the far end of the corridor. "It's the elevator. I'm quite sure I didn't send it back up."

"Must be the Batman," she said. "Looks like he's home early." She seemed delighted at the prospect.

"No," said Alfred, "not this early. Not when . . ."

The elevator was coming back down.

"Quickly," said Alfred, "get out to the cave and hide!"

He ran toward the door of the armory and flung it open. He grabbed a Walther P38 semiautomatic off the wall and ran across the room toward the ammunition locker, fumbling with his keys. He found the right key and inserted it into the lock. He flung open the door of the cabinet and took out a box of 9mm ammo, then jacked the magazine out of the Walther and quickly started inserting the rounds into it.

"Mr. Pennyworth, I presume?" said a voice from the door.

Alfred spun around, trying to insert the half-filled magazine into the pistol at the same time.

Specter fired.

The bullet from the .45 Winchester Magnum took him in the right shoulder and flung him back against the wall. The pistol and magazine dropped from his hands as he fell to the floor.

"My, my," Specter said as he came into the room, "what a lethal collection you have here. Quite an arsenal, indeed."

He glanced at the weapons on the walls. "I've always wanted one of these," he said, taking down an autoloading rifle. It was a state-of-the-art Austrian assault rifle with a forty-two-round magazine and a futuristic-looking, one-piece, molded synthetic stock and scope mount. It had a laser-beam sight attached to it. "Very nice," he said. "Very nice, indeed."

He walked over to the ammunition locker and picked out a box of .223 ammo. He holstered his pistol and started to load the rifle magazine.

"Where is the witness, Mr. Pennyworth?" he asked casually as he inserted the rounds into the magazine.

"You . . . go to the . . . devil!" Alfred gasped.

Specter clucked his tongue. "Ah, yes. That old S.A.S.

spirit. Well, you're not in the commandos now, my friend. And I am not some bog-trotting Provo."

"No, you're worse..." gasped Alfred. "You're a... bloody... butcher."

"Now, that's rather unkind, considering I could have killed you straight away," Specter said. "I'm going to have to kill you anyway, but if you insist on being difficult, I can take my time about it."

"Do your worst... damn you!"

Specter smiled. "You're a tough old man, aren't you?" he said. "I like that. Perhaps I'll kill you quickly. Only not yet. Not until your employer returns. What was it he said? He would drag me out from under whatever rock I was hiding beneath? Something like that, wasn't it? A very colorful speech, as I recall. Well, it seems that I am not the one hiding beneath rocks. What do you say we take a look around at this famous Batcave of yours? I've been looking forward to seeing it. Get up."

Alfred remained on the floor.

"I said *get up*," said Specter, giving him a vicious kick. "Or would you rather I shot your ear off?"

He aimed the rifle down at Alfred's head.

"You... barbarian," said Alfred, struggling to get up. Specter watched him without offering any assistance.

"Yes, I am not a gentleman, I'm afraid," he said. "Sorry if that offends your sensibilities, but there it is. And if you're thinking of trying any heroics with your one good arm, please don't. I would hate to shoot you again and have you bleed to death before Wayne returns. That would rather spoil the surprise."

He shoved Alfred out ahead of him, into the corridor. The big .45 Winchester Magnum slug, fired at such close range, had penetrated Alfred's shoulder completely, with hardly any expansion, but it had still made a nasty wound and Alfred was bleeding badly. He stumbled on ahead, barely able to stand on his feet.

Specter checked the other doors, then prodded Alfred toward the door at the far end of the corridor, leading into the central control room of the Batcave. Once inside, he gave a low whistle.

"Very impressive," he said. "It's unfortunate that I haven't time for the complete tour. I would very much like to know more about some of this equipment." He glanced out through the glass walls of the control room. "Very impressive, indeed. Quite astonishing that you were able to keep all this a secret. My admiration for your employer is growing by leaps and bounds. It's really too bad I'll have to kill him. There is probably much I could have learned from him."

"You will learn . . . a great deal . . . before the night is out," said Alfred, leaning against one of the consoles for support.

"Yes, well, I'm sure one of us will," said Specter. "Now then, where is our witness hiding?"

"I wouldn't tell you . . . if I knew," said Alfred.

"No, I don't imagine that you would," said Specter. "The question was rhetorical. No matter. At least we know it's not in here. Out in the cavern somewhere. Undoubtedly, there are countless nooks and crannies in which one may hide. But I am very good at looking." He kept Alfred covered as he opened the door leading out into the cavern. "After you," he said, gesturing with his weapon.

Alfred stumbled through the door. He was getting

weak from loss of blood and his vision was starting to blur.

"Now then," Specter said, "let's see where your elusive guest is." He stood at the top of the stairs cut into the rock formation, above the floor, and called out to the cavern, "I know you're down there. If you come out, I will make it quick and relatively painless. If you make me come and look for you, I will not be so charitable."

Summoning all his strength, Alfred yelled out, "Stay where you are, Rachel! Don't listen to him!"

Specter glanced at him sharply. "Rachel?"

She stepped out from behind a large stalagmite on the cavern floor. "Leave him alone, Eric," she called out to him. "It's me you want."

Specter stared at her with astonishment. "*Rachel? You're* the witness against Garcia?"

"Yeah," she said, standing below him, about fifty feet away. "How's that for a kick in the head?"

"I heard you were dead."

"You heard wrong."

"Why?" he asked her. "Why are you doing this?"

"What difference does it make?" she asked. "What do you care? East Berlin was a long time ago."

"Yes," he said. "Yes, it was." He sighed. "Something told me I never should have taken this job."

"But you're gonna do it anyway, aren't you?" she said.

"I accepted the contract," he said. "I have no choice."

"That's what I figured," she said. "You always were a cold son of a bitch."

"So it was you," he said. "That's how the Batman got such a good description of me."

"You've changed your face," she said. "But you always were fond of your pretty white hair. As white as snow. Cold, pristine and pure. That's you to a T, isn't it, Eric? If that's really your name."

"As a matter of fact, it is," he said. "It's a pity things could not have turned out differently for us. I was very fond of you."

"Fond?" she said, bitterly. "I loved you, you bastard. I would've died for you."

"I'm afraid you will," he said.

"Rachel, no!" shouted Alfred. "Run!"

"Be quiet, old man," said Specter. "There is nowhere for her to run, and she knows it."

"Why don't you just do it, Eric, and get it over with?" said Rachel. "You already killed me, back when you left me in Berlin. So go ahead and finish the damn job."

"I had intended to wait until your protector returned," he said, "so that I could have the satisfaction of seeing his face when I did it. But for old times' sake, the least I can do is to be quick and merciful."

"You want me to move closer and make it easier for you?" she spat at him.

"No need," he replied, calmly. "I can easily make the shot from here. Just stand still and I'll make it as painless as possible. Just one shot, right between the eyes. It will be over before you know it."

He raised the Steyr rifle. The laser beam lanced out toward her, making a red dot just above the bridge of her nose.

"Goodbye, Rachel..."

"No!" shouted Alfred, throwing himself at the assassin. They both fell and the shot went wild. Alfred lunged

away, rolling painfully down the stone steps cut into the rock formation, down to the cavern floor.

"That was very foolish," said Specter, getting back up to his feet. "All you succeeded in doing was momentarily delaying the inevitable."

"No, he bought me the time I needed," a deep, resonant voice called out echoing through the cavern.

Specter glanced sharply toward the sound. The Batman stood atop a rock formation across the cavern from him, near the stone steps leading down from the entrance through the grandfather clock. In his dark, flowing black cape and ominous-looking cowl, he resembled a specter himself.

"You!" said Specter. He raised his rifle and fired, but the slug failed to penetrate the Kevlar panels sewn into the Batman's cape. With a deft, quick motion, the Batman hurled a batarang. It whistled through the air and Specter barely succeeded in deflecting it with the barrel of the rifle. The Batman dropped down behind the rock formation, out of sight.

"You are on *my* territory now, Specter," he called out. "By the way, that bomb you planted tonight was found and by now it's been disabled. You've killed for the last time."

"I think not," said Specter. He dropped down to the cavern floor and rolled with the impact, keeping a secure grip on the rifle.

Alfred, gritting his teeth against the pain and fighting to keep from lapsing into unconsciousness, scrambled toward Rachel.

"You're hurt!" she said.

"Never mind . . . that," he gasped. "We've got to . . . get

you to the Batmobile and... lock you in! It's impregnable. Armor-plated... glass is bulletproof...."

"Come on," she said, "lean on me."

"I will deal with you presently, old man!" Specter called out.

"You will deal with me *now*!" the Batman said, and a gas pellet exploded almost at the assassin's feet. He lunged away from it and rolled, holding his breath, getting away from the spreading cloud of gas, which dissipated rapidly in the openness of the cavern.

"Nice try!" shouted Specter. "But not quite good enough. You're not dealing with an amateur now. That silly costume of yours might frighten a common criminal, but it merely amuses me. And your little tricks and gadgets will not save you."

There was no reply.

"What, nothing to say?" Specter called out, moving stealthily across the cavern floor, using the rock formations as cover. "I thought you were going to step on me. Put me in jail, isn't that what you said?"

Alfred and Rachel reached the Batmobile, with her supporting him by bracing his good arm across her shoulders. "Inside... quickly!" he said.

"What about you?"

"Don't... worry... about... me," he gasped, closing the door after she got in. With Rachel locked inside, nothing short of a bomb would get to her, he thought, and Specter had exploded his last bomb. Now, if he could only get to... He managed to make five more steps before he collapsed, unconscious.

The red beam of the laser sight swept the rock formations in the shadows at the rear of the main chamber of the cavern.

"Where is your bravado now, Wayne?" Specter called out.

"You want me?" the Batman called out. "Come and get me. If you dare."

He was drawing Specter deeper into the cavern system, away from Alfred and Rachel. His first concern was for their safety, to make sure they were out of any possible line of fire. The red beam of the laser sight touched his shoulder briefly, and he darted back just as the bullet spanged into the rocks beside him.

"A little close for comfort, was it?" Specter called out.

"You'll have to do better than that, butcher," the Batman replied.

"I'm enjoying this, Wayne," Specter called out, moving closer, following him deeper into the cavern. "You hear me?"

"All I hear is hot air."

Specter chuckled. "After I've taken care of you, I'll see to the others," he called out. "And then I will have your head delivered to Commissioner James Gordon in a box, wrapped up with a pretty ribbon."

Specter fired again, twice. One of the bullets whizzed past the Batman's head, missing it by centimeters; the other one struck the rock he was using for shelter, chipping it and lacerating his cheek with the fragments. The sounds of the shots and the ricochets echoed through the cavern.

They had left the lighted area now and were in total darkness. "Can you see in the dark, Wayne, like your namesake?'' Specter called out. "I can. How thoughtful of you to provide me with a nightscope."

The Batman reached into his utility belt and pulled out the sections of a small pair of infrared goggles. He snapped them together, attached the strap, and slipped them on over his cowl. He could not see the assassin. Specter was moving carefully but steadily toward him, using all available natural cover. Using only the nightscope, he could fire without giving himself away, but if he used the laser sight, which made it easier to pinpoint his target, there would be an instant in which the thin, tightly collimated red beam would give away his location. He would be making his movements carefully, then checking through the nightscope to sweep the area around him. And that could be used against him.

"How far does this cavern extend, Wayne?" Specter called out, his voice echoing in the darkness. "The tunnel appears to be narrowing. Does it end in a cul-de-sac? In a passageway too small to squeeze through? Are you starting to feel frightened, Wayne?"

The Batman stopped at a wide fissure in the tunnel wall. He squeezed into it, then began to "chimney" his way up, climbing up inside the fissure by bracing himself against one side with his back and inching upward with his feet and hands.

"Where are you, Wayne?" Specter called out. "What are you doing? Are you saying your prayers?"

Above them, the bats were chittering loudly and flitting about in all directions, disturbed by the sounds of the gunfire. He was now well above the tunnel floor, and he could go no farther. The fissure had grown too narrow. He braced himself tightly and reached for his utility belt.

He took out a slender tube that resembled a large and elongated brass cylinder casing for a bullet; but this object was made of plastic, and crimped into the end of it was a barbed, titanium dart. He drew out a line from the spool in his belt and clipped it to the dart head.

The tunnel ended not in a cul-de-sac but in a wide crevice, a deep fissure in the cavern floor, the one that had taken the life of one of his ancestors. He was trapped between Specter and the crevice. And the assassin was not going to run out of ammunition anytime soon.

From this height, he could look down at the tunnel floor and see Specter through his goggles, cautiously moving forward, checking every few seconds through his nightscope. He had spotted the area to his left, where a wide rock ledge jutted out over the tunnel floor, and he was making his way toward it, hoping to get above his quarry, not realizing that his quarry was already above him. The Batman tensed, waiting, using all his strength to keep himself propped up high in the fissure of the wall. "Come on, Specter," he whispered under his breath. "Let's have another of your mocking taunts."

"It's over Wayne!" Specter called out. "You have nowhere left to run!"

As he spoke, the Batman held the tube out away from him, aiming it toward the opposite wall of the tunnel, and pressed down hard on the firing stud with his thumb. There was a silenced chuffing sound, masked by the sound of Specter's voice and the mad chittering of the bats in the darkness. The titanium dart flew across the tunnel, trailing the slender line behind it as it unwound rapidly from the spool inside his belt, and embedded itself in the opposite wall.

Specter was climbing up onto the ledge on the opposite side, just below him. The Batman wound the line around his wrist, then pressed a button on the spool housing that snipped the rest of the line from the spool. Bracing himself, he reached with his free hand into another compartment of his utility belt and pulled out several flare pellets.

Specter was atop the ledge now, silent, so as not to give away what he thought was his superior position. He was sweeping the tunnel floor below him with the rifle, looking through the nightscope.

The Batman slipped the night goggles down around his neck and tossed the pellets.

The flares exploded in a blinding white light, illuminating the entire tunnel. The bats went crazy. Specter, who had been looking through his nightscope when the flares went off, recoiled from it with a cry, momentarily blinded, and he didn't see the Batman come swinging down across the tunnel toward him, his cape billowing out behind him as he brought his legs forward, feet out, to increase his momentum. He struck the assassin in the chest with his feet, knocking him backward, but Specter managed to retain his grip on the rifle. The bats were darting madly all over the cavern, their shrieks filling the air.

Specter struck the ground and rolled, coming up fast, still seeing sparks in front of his eyes as the Batman came at him. He swung out hard with the butt of his rifle and caught the Batman a glancing blow on the chin. The Batman staggered, recovered, and then Specter was bringing the rifle around to fire. The Batman made a flying dive to one side as the bullets passed over him; he rolled, then hurled a razorwing, but the moment he realized he'd missed his shots, Specter moved with incredible swiftness. The assassin executed a diving forward roll toward the Batman and came up with his rifle at high port, swinging it at the Batman's chin.

The Batman blocked the rifle with his forearm and then delivered a hard undercut aimed at the assassin's solar plexus, but Specter brought the rifle down, using the stock like a fighting staff, and blocked the blow. He immediately struck out with the butt around again, aiming for the Batman's temple, but the Batman dropped to the ground and executed a sweep, knocking the assassin's legs out from under him. Still retaining a hold on his weapon, Specter fell, but rolled backward slightly and executed a kick-up, leaping nimbly to his feet once more, with the rifle in position to fire. The Batman kicked it out of his hands and it flew through the air, to land near the lip of the rock ledge, above the precipice.

Specter executed a lightning-fast, spinning back kick, which the Batman ducked beneath. But before he could counter with a strike of his own, Specter was launching a front kick at his groin. Using an aikido move, the Batman swept his arm around underneath the kick and grabbed the assassin's heel, yanking upward, forcing the momentum of the kick to continue and throw him over backward, but Specter turned it into a back somersault and landed on his feet. Mere seconds had passed since they first started their combat, but the light from the flares was fading rapidly and the bats were flocking all over the place, driven to a frenzy by the light and all the activity. Specter continued the back somersault with a back handspring, which brought him closer to the fallen rifle. The Batman quickly reached for his utility belt, but Specter saw the move and in one smooth, quick motion, he unsheathed his knife and threw it, and then immediately drew his pistol.

The Batman jerked his head aside at the last instant and the knife flew past him harmlessly, but he saw the big Grizzly coming up and barely had time to wrap his Kevlar-paneled cape around himself before it went off. The big .45 Magnum slug struck the Kevlar-panels in his cape, but they were not strong enough to withstand such a powerful round. The bullet penetrated, but was sufficiently slowed that the protective bat emblem on his chest was able to stop it. However, the 230-grain jacketed bullet traveling at over 1,600 feet per second packed a wallop that knocked him right off his feet, stunning him.

Specter holstered the pistol and picked up the assault rifle, with its larger magazine of high-velocity .223 ammo. The light from the flare pellets was now almost completely gone. As the Batman lay, stunned, Specter activated the laser sight and placed the red dot of the beam right over the Batman's stomach.

"I've got about thirty rounds left," he said with a cold smile. "Let's see how many you can take before you die."

But before he could squeeze the trigger, a maddened bat flew right into his face. He cried out, dropping the rifle and backing up involuntarily as he brought his hands up to tear it away, and he went over the edge.

The last sparking embers of the flare pellets died away, plunging everything into total darkness. With a moan, the Batman propped himself up and drew a deep breath. The bat that had flown into Specter's face darted past him.

"Thanks, friend," he said.

He reached down and pulled the night goggles up from around his neck and over his eyes again. Rubbing his chest, he made his way over to the lip of the ledge. There were faint sounds coming from below. He glanced down.

Specter was about twenty feet below him, hanging over the crevice, clinging to a rock outcropping.

"Hold on!" the Batman called down to him. "I'll throw you a line!"

He unwound a length of the strong, nylon filament line from the spool in his belt, weighted it with a clamp, and started to lower it to the assassin. Specter was in total darkness, and Batman knew he couldn't see.

"It's coming down toward you," he called down.

Then, as the Batman watched with utter disbelief, the assassin drew his Grizzly from its shoulder holster and, hanging on with one hand, started to raise it, aiming for the sound of his voice.

"Don't be a fool!" the Batman shouted. "Drop the gun and grab the line!"

Specter fired.

The bullet whizzed past the Batman's head like an angry hornet, and the recoil of the big .45 Mag made Specter lose his grip. He fell down into the crevice, screaming with defiant rage, holding the big Grizzly in both hands and continuing to fire up at the Batman as he fell, emptying the magazine. One of the bullets plucked at the Batman's cape as he jerked back away from the ledge, his jaw slack in astonishment. Specter's echoing scream died away into the distance.

"Why?" the Batman said to himself, stunned.

And the answer came to him, in the form of a memory

of a fable he'd read as a child. It was the fable of the frog and the scorpion. The scorpion wanted to cross the pond, and he asked the frog to give him a ride. The frog, distrustful, refused, afraid that the scorpion would sting him.

"But if I do," the scorpion replied, "then we shall both drown."

That made sense to the frog, and he agreed to ride the scorpion across. But halfway across the pond, the scorpion stung the frog.

"But *why*?" the frog said as the lethal poison began to do its work. "Now you'll die too! *Why did you sting me?*"

And an instant before the waters closed over its head, the scorpion replied, "Because it is my nature."

EPILOGUE

THE Batmobile was already waiting for them when Commissioner Gordon and Agent Chambers pulled into the overlook just off the highway. Across the river, the lights of Gotham City and the Gotham Bridge could be seen sparkling in the distance. As Gordon and Chambers got out of the car, the doors of the Batmobile opened and the Batman stepped out with Rachel Morrison.

"As promised, Mr. Chambers," he said. "I am delivering the witness safe and sound."

"Much obliged, Batman," said Chambers. "Ms. Morrison," he added, nodding to her.

She glanced back at the Batman. He nodded. "Good luck with your second chance, Rachel," he said.

She bit her lower lip, then ran back to him and kissed him on the cheek. Then she went quickly toward the car that Chambers and Gordon came in without looking back. She was afraid she would start crying.

"It's been interesting," said Chambers, holding out his hand. The Batman took it. "All charges have been dropped by the way. The Bureau's grateful."

"My pleasure, Mr. Chambers. Just make sure that Garcia gets put away for a long time."

"We'll see to that," said Chambers. "He's already singing like a bird to the Justice Department. And with what he's giving us, we're going to be able to hurt the Macros bad. Maybe even put 'em out of business, at least in this country."

"I'm glad to hear that."

"Take care of yourself, Batman," Chambers said.

"You too, Mr. Chambers."

He went back toward the car. Gordon lingered. "How's Alfred Pennyworth?" he asked.

"Recovering nicely," said the Batman. "I spoke to the hospital earlier this afternoon and he should be out by tomorrow, although he'll have to do some physical therapy for a while."

"He was very lucky you arrived in time," said Gordon. "And it was a lucky thing for Bruce Wayne that he wasn't home. It never occurred to us that Specter might target individual wealthy and influential citizens of Gotham City. Sadly, we weren't able to get to David Jacks in time. But at least Specter paid for his crimes with his life."

"Yes," said the Batman, "although I wish I could have taken him alive."

"He actually committed suicide rather than be captured," Gordon said, shaking his head. That was what the Batman had told him, without elaborating on the details, and essentially it was the truth. "I suppose it's just as well. I don't imagine he would have lasted very long in prison, unless he was confined to solitary. When I think of all the lives that were lost because of him..."

"Yes, I know," the Batman said. "It grieves me deeply. It will be a long time before the wounds of this city can heal."

"Already, there are people in the media asking if the whole thing was worth it," Gordon said, "suggesting that all those lives could have been saved if we'd simply released Garcia, or if the government never seized him in the first place."

"If they had done that," the Batman said, "then they would have left themselves at the mercy of every thug with a gun or bomb in the entire world. People like that cannot be negotiated with, and their methods must never be allowed to succeed, because if that were to happen, the cost in human lives would be even greater. And we would continue paying it. As for people like Garcia and the Macros, who declare war on this country of ours and fight it with drugs and terrorism, they need to be treated just the same as if they had invaded us with armies. Which, in effect, is exactly what they've done."

"You don't have to convince me," said Gordon. "But I wish you could convince the media."

"It's the people who count," the Batman said. "In times of crisis, they can pull together, as we have seen. They know who their enemies are."

"And who their friends are, too," said Gordon, holding out his hand to the Batman. They shook. "Take care of yourself, my friend."

"You too, Jim. Just remember, when you need me, I'll be there."

* * *

Enrique Vasquez pulled the bright red Porsche into his spot in the underground parking garage of his luxury apartment building on Gotham City's trendy Upper East Side. Sitting in the passenger seat beside him was a stunningly ethereal, leggy blonde whose mind, in his opinion, had never been sullied by the presence of an original thought. Not that he really cared. She was an absolutely gorgeous creature, with a lovely, heart-shaped face and big blue eyes, and if her conversation was limited to expressions such as "How totally fascinating!" and "Oh, wow!", he didn't mind a bit, because he was the one she found "totally fascinating" and all he could think of when he stared at those incredible long legs was "Oh, wow!"

"So, like, this is where you live, huh?" she said, as he turned off the motor.

"Up on the fifteenth floor," he replied. "I can't wait to see what you think of the place. I've got it decorated with mementoes of my career, photographs of me with celebrities I've interviewed, awards, a portrait of me done by Andy Warhol, stuff like that."

"How totally fascinating!"

"Yeah, I figure we can have some wine, put on some mellow music, turn the lights down low and spend a little time getting to know each other."

She smiled, "I'd like that."

So would I, thought Vasquez, as he got out of the car and came around to open the door for her, so that he could receive the full benefit of her short skirt hiking up those long legs as she got out of the low-built Porsche. The car was worth every penny he paid for it, he thought, just for the way women got in and out of it.

As they came around the rear of the car, the twin beams

of a pair of blindingly bright headlights suddenly came on and struck them, from a sleek black car that had come silently coasting down the ramp behind them. As Vasquez flinched and shielded his eyes, a large, dark figure stepped out in front of the headlights, silhouetted in their glow.

"Good evening, Mr. Vasquez," said a deep, resonant voice.

Vasquez saw the flowing cape and the large, pointed ears on the dark cowl and he involuntarily took several steps back.

"Batman!" he said.

"Oh, wow!" said the blonde.

"Good evening, Miss," said the Batman. "I wonder if you'd mind stepping over here for a moment. I'd like a private word with Mr. Vasquez."

"You stay right here," said Vasquez, reaching out for her, but she was already moving toward the Batman.

"Would you care to wait inside the Batmobile?" the Batman said to her. "Just don't touch any switches. It could be dangerous."

"Oh, wow!"

"What do you want?" demanded Vasquez, nervously.

"I thought we might have a short discussion," said the Batman, moving closer. "About journalistic integrity."

Vasquez stepped back. "Just don't come any closer," he said, his voice cracking slightly. "I . . . I've studied martial arts."

"Have you now?" said the Batman, with a smile. He continued to come closer.

"Look, I . . . I don't want any trouble," Vasquez said, his voice trembling slightly as he backed away.

"For someone who doesn't want any trouble, you've

certainly caused more than your share," the Batman replied, still moving toward him as Vasquez backed away.

"Hey, I'm a reporter," Vasquez said, defensively, as he continued to back away. "I just report the news."

"No, Enrique," said the Batman, "you're far less interested in reporting news than in making news. There is a difference, you know."

"Look... you stay away from me!" said Vasquez, backing up until he hit the wall. He glanced around quickly from side to side, searching for a means of escape. "I've got my rights! I've got no quarrel with you!"

"Oh, but I'm afraid that *I* have a quarrel with *you*," the Batman replied. "I have a quarrel with your grandstanding self-promotion at the expense of the people who try to keep law and order in this city. I have a quarrel with the way you hide behind the First Amendment in order to showboat for the camera and magnify your own pathetic sense of self-importance. I have a quarrel with the way you use the media as a tool to satisfy your over-inflated ego while withholding important evidence from the police and catering to the twisted needs of a homicidal maniac..."

"Look, okay," said Vasquez, swallowing hard, "okay, maybe I went too far, but I was only trying to do my job. Look... maybe we can work something out."

"Oh? What would you suggest?"

"I could make you a star," said Vasquez, quickly. "I could do a series of reports on you, play up that you're a hero, and not some dangerous vigilante. Anything you want, you just tell me how to play it. I didn't mean to cause you any trouble, honest, I didn't! I'll make it up to you, okay? It could work out for both of us. You scratch my back and I'll scratch yours. Anything you want, man, just don't hurt me, please!"

"Have you got that, Miss Williams?" said the Batman.

"I've got it," Connie Williams said, stepping out into the light with her cameraman.

Vasquez glanced quickly from Batman to her and back again. "What the hell is this?" he said.

"The real Enrique Vasquez," said the newswoman, with a smile, "up close and personal."

"You've got that all on tape?" said Vasquez, with dismay.

"Every groveling word and gesture," she replied.

"You can't use that!" he said. "You can't put that on the air!"

"No, maybe not," she said, "but I can make copies and pass them around to every station in the city, for the private enjoyment of the *real* reporters in this town. And we can play it at parties, where some of your celebrity friends that you're always toadying up to can see you in action. "I'll make you a star," she mimicked. "Just don't hurt me, please!"

"Connie! Connie, you can't *do* this!"

"Wanna bet? Watch me. Thanks, Batman. I owe you one."

"Anytime, Miss Williams. Goodnight, Mr. Vasquez," said the Batman.

"Connie! Connie, wait!"

"Can I give you a lift somewhere, Miss?" Vasquez heard the Batman ask the leggy blond.

"A ride in the Batmobile? Oh, *wow!*"

ABOUT THE AUTHOR

Simon Hawke has been a full-time writer for more than a dozen years. He is the author of over forty novels, ranging from science fiction and fantasy to historical fiction. An avid motorcyclist and pistol shooter, his interests also include martial arts, horseback riding and music. He is a former rock drummer and "a fairly incompetent guitarist".

He has also been a radio announcer and engineer, a custom motorcycle builder, a bartender, an armed guard and "a host of other peculiar occupations". As a boy, he followed Batman's adventures in Detective Comics and never dreamed he would one day wind up writing about the caped crusader. He currently lives in Colorado.